1 —

Mangos, Bananas and Coconuts: A Cuban Love Story

Himilce Novas

Arte Público Press
Houston, Texas
1996

This volume is made possible through grants from the National Endowment for the Arts (a federal agency) and the Andrew W. Mellon Foundation.

Recovering the past, creating the future

Arte Público Press
University of Houston
Houston, Texas 77204-2090

Cover art by Christina Gonzalez
Cover design by Gladys Ramirez

Novas, Himilce.
    Mangos, bananas and coconuts: a Cuban love story / by Himilce Novas.
        p.   cm.
    ISBN 1-55885-092-9 (cloth : alk. paper)
    1. Man-woman relationships—Cuba—Fiction. 2. Twins—United States—Fiction. 3. Cuban Americans—Fiction. I. Title.
PS3564.O9147M36   1996
813'.54—dc20   95-37661
                                                              CIP

The paper used in this publication meets the requirements of the American National Standard for Permanence of Paper for Printed Library Materials Z39.48-1984. ∞

To her for whom it was written

"And now good morrow to our waking lives"
John Donne

Mangos, Bananas and Coconuts: A Cuban Love Story

One

This is a story about a woman named Esmeralda Saavedra, a Cuban, according to her father, a Hispanic according to the Census, and a New Yorker, as she first called herself before she found a need to cling to her identity by its roots and follicles, and thus call herself Cuban again, who at twenty-nine sealed her fate by falling in love, and then having fallen in love, committed a foolish act to rectify her mistake.

And it is equally the story of Juan—or Don Juan, as his schoolmates at Yale dubbed him— Esmeralda's twin brother, who could not let his sister be and thus was said to have committed first the act of salmon swimming upstream and then that of lemmings hurling themselves into a waterfall or a high diver plunging into an empty pool.

How it began: some might say it began in Cuba, in 1958, one year before Fidel Castro came down from the mountains. An apocalyptic horseman on a Jeep, he wore jet and mother-of-pearl rosaries twisted around his Galician-Spanish neck and into his gnarled and prickly Lebanese beard. 1958 was the year Arnaldo, Juan and Esmeralda's father, was visited by the Southern Methodist missionaries passing through Santiago de Cuba in Oriente province. Arnaldo worked there at the Ingenio Ona—a sugar plantation that spread so deep and wide that Arnaldo had believed until only a few years before this encounter with the Lord that the *ingenio* was all there was and that a man could travel a thousand leagues out from the center of the land and not reach the rest of Cuba until he found himself smack in the middle of the Cathedral of Havana, staring at the plaster Jesus hanging from the ceiling, with mahogany blood clotted along the sides of his skinny ribs and his tapeworm belly.

And that year Arnaldo found himself in the middle of a revival, a crusade led by a freckled, orange-haired young minister from the town of Florence, Alabama, on the border of Tennessee. Arnaldo, who was just sixteen himself, walked to the front of the makeshift altar of palm tree *guano* and wooden crates used to ship the sugar cane to the U.S., and gave his life to Jesus, singing *Jesus, Jesus, Jesus, Sweetest Name I Know/Jesus, Jesus, Jesus, Keeps Me Singing As I Go*. He did not know what he was saying, since those had been the first words he'd ever uttered in a tongue that, by one of the many twists of fate that knotted his strange and winding road, would be the language he'd be destined—other exiles said condemned—to hear all around him for the rest of his life.

What Arnaldo felt and why he gave his life to Jesus had been the subject of much speculation among the *guajiros*, the native peasants, many blond and blue-eyed, whose ancestors, known as *Guanches*, had come to Cuba from the Canary Islands and who were known for their common sense and, some said, their stubborn-as-a-mule and dogged-as-a-dog way of seeing things for what they were and not for what at first the priests and later the politicians swore up and down they were.

"You mean to tell me," Perfecto, his first cousin and only living relative, had told him, "that just because you walk up there and stare at that speckled runt of a guinea hen shouting and waving his arms and you tell him you *personally* accept Jesus, you won't have any more debts to pay for the rest of your life? How do you know that *Americano* can possibly be so rich as to take care of this whole crowd? And what could he possibly want with you, an orphan without a pot to piss in, a man who is not even man enough to get a *compañera* of the female sex to call himself a man with?"

And Arnaldo had tried to explain, although he had not yet been able to reason it out to himself, that the orange-haired man was talking about a different kind of debt, a debt that had more to do with

the worthless scum he was than what he owed the
bodega in the mill for rum.

Ever since he could remember looking up from
the dirt floor and crawling in his dead grandmother's tin- and thatched-roof hut in the back of the
Casa Grande of the Ingenio Ona, sucking little
pieces of lime rock and colored marbles and rolling
them around in his mouth because he was always
so hungry, ever since then, even before he was a
total orphan, he had truly believed he was scum
and the shit that comes out of goats in the field in
little hard pebbles that later stink as much as cow
dung. And because of this, because of what and who
he was, his debt in the world was very great, un-
bearably great.

Arnaldo had never discussed these thoughts
with anyone who knew more than he did. For if he
had, the visit from the missionary from Florence,
Alabama, might have cast a different dye on that
strange and winding road called his life.

Soon after Arnaldo gave his life to Jesus, the
tongues began wagging and the gossip got more
twisted than the cyclone of 1944 that had left the
guajiros alone and naked, wondering how to make a
town from scratch that had just grown so naturally
over the years since the Spanish first landed, or at
least since 1792 when slave shipments increased
from Africa and a new wave of Spanish immigrants
from Galicia and the Canary Islands came to Cuba.

What got the gossip started was the way Arnaldo's life suddenly changed after the fateful Saturday at the altar when he turned the palms of his hands to the still, flesh-of-coconut moon that hung over Cuba and sang *Jesus, Jesus, Jesus, Sweetest Name I Know*. Perfecto said that Arnaldo had become a different man. Other laborers at the Ingenio Ona said that a miracle had definitely taken place, but could only explain it by saying that Arnaldo had become a lucky man, even a lucky charm, a man who could bring luck to others if his body happened to touch them or his breath or spit mingled with theirs.

And this is how it happened. First, to describe Arnaldo before he was born-again was to call him a lanky youth with oily pores, a gaunt face like Don Quijote's, and hazel eyes the color of dusty plums. For a sixteen-year old of Galician Spanish descent, he was practically hairless. If other young men of his same ancestry shaved twice a day, Arnaldo only needed to rake off the little straggly hair on his cheeks and the corners of his lips twice a week. If other young men sang baritone and carried deep-throated conversations with other threshers so far down the line that they looked like lady bugs in the sun, Arnaldo sounded like the *voce bianche* of the Vatican, or as his grandmother had told him before she died of a strangulated hernia, like a mule with tiny testicles.

Only a few days after Arnaldo gave his life to Jesus—the wagging tongues said it happened over-night with the rising of the sun—this lanky and hairless young man burst from his chrysalis like a mutant and monstrous butterfly. His face became full and his cinder skin turned the texture of golden mangos. His hair, suddenly black and thick and shiny with a rich anointing, spread like a mangled grove across his strong, muscular arms and legs and thighs and manly chest. And those who had seen him taking a leak on a coconut tree at siesta time swore his member had shot up to half the size of his sharp, lethal *machete*. His teeth, too, had ben-efited from the general shine that had come over his head. They got suddenly straight and pearly, and the two that were missing—one up top and one in the bottom—grew back. And all the gaps in his mouth were filled, and the yellow and black little holes, from eating sugar with coffee and coffee with sugar all day, were gone.

Arnaldo did not seem to have noticed his sud-den change—at least he didn't speak of it to the rest of the *guajiros*. He continued his usual routine in the mill, cutting cane in the morning and stacking the stalks in the open carts in the evening. The real miracle, in his eyes, was the fact that he was able to read the pocket-size books the orange-haired mis-sionary had left him, along with an illustrated, bilingual edition of the King James Bible in large print, with Jesus' words in red boldface. This was awesome to Arnaldo because he had never learned to read more than a few words. (He could make out *peligro*—danger—and *pesos*—Cuban dollars—and *Mejoral*—a brand name for aspirin that was advertised on the door of the country store—because his dead grandmother had drilled it into him.) And now, suddenly, by the grace of Jesus the Lord, he was reading as swiftly as a politician who had gone, if not to the University of Havana, at least to the University of Santiago de Cuba. What's more, he could read the English pages on the right side of the Bible like he was Mickey Mantle's long lost brother.

Arnaldo admired Mickey Mantle. Perfecto had read him articles about the American baseball hero and showed him Mantle's picture in the Santiago paper. Arnaldo's new linguistic ability made him think that he was destined to meet Mickey some day, speak with him in his own tongue, become friends, even be invited to a ball game in Yankee Stadium and afterwards go out with him for a glass of thin American beer.

The sure sign that something truly amazing had happened to Arnaldo was the fact that the other workers spoke more about him than with him. And when they addressed him, they squinted or averted their eyes and made feeble attempts at bowing, even if in the back of their minds they still kept thinking of him as that orphan, that tapeworm runt of the litter, that illiterate peasant who was not exactly one of them but even less than one of them. Still, they wanted to touch him, or stand downwind of his breath, or even on a couple of occasions steal his sweaty undershirts and jute-sack trunks and tuck them under their children's pillows for good luck.

Arnaldo seemed unaware of all the commotion on his account. He spent most nights reading his Bible by the oil lamp in his grandmother's hut, reciting the Beatitudes and drawing pictures in his mind of Jesus walking through the sugar mill wearing a starchy brand-new *guayabera* and smoking a Cuban cigar, talking to Arnaldo and Mickey Mantle and President Fulgencio Batista, as well as Matthew, Mark, Luke and John. He sang a hymn the missionary had taught him, over and over again, in English and Spanish—*And He walks with me and He talks with me and He tells me I am His own*—and he stopped counting how many hours he slept, or if he slept at all.

Once, Perfecto came to see him in the middle of the night, hell-bent on finding out what his first cousin had done to change himself into an entirely different-looking man—a strong and handsome man at that. When he looked through the window, he discovered Arnaldo in deep conversation with a large plumed owl and a three-legged donkey with eyes in the back of its neck. Perfecto ran home and hid in the stinky out-house, holding his nose and breathing through his mouth until the moon sank in the field and the first mockingbird sang out loud. He didn't dare tell anyone what he had seen for fear of what might happen to him and his family for spying on this witchman who still called him *primo*— cousin—and chopped cane with him side by side under the searing sun.

Then came the day when Arnaldo was called to try his mettle, just like the orange-haired missionary had preached, just like Jesus was called for his first miracle: the very difficult task of turning water into wine.

It happened when the polio epidemic struck Oriente province like a hurricane. Women and children and even grown men were turning into cripples overnight. The disease struck everyone: rich people and poor people, the foremen, common laborers, the plantation owners. A cadre of *campesinos* who had been helping Fidel in the Sierra Maestra mountains not far from the Ona Sugar Mill had spread the word that the Yankees—not the baseball team Arnaldo followed, but the *Americanos*, or as Fidel called them, *Yanquis*—had brought vials of polio germs which Dwight Eisenhower had extracted from the corpse of President Franklin Delano Roosevelt. The Yankees were infecting the people of Cuba, particularly those of Oriente province to keep them from overthrowing Batista, the *Yanqui* puppet.

Perfecto's young daughter, Ermenegilda, was the first victim at the sugar mill. The tiny eight-year old was running a fever so high that dunking her in the brook in the middle of the night, or applying compresses of mint leaves, or covering her frail little body with ravenous leeches just left her pale and barely conscious. As a last resort, Don Mario Ona, the owner of the mill, had reluctantly summoned a doctor to save Perfecto's little Ermenegilda. But the girl grew weaker, and soon she was throwing up even the tiny spoonfuls of synthetic medicine the doctor from the capital had prescribed.

On the day he was called to witness, Arnaldo was sitting in front of his hut on his dead grandmother's cane rocking chair, fanning himself with a giant *uva caleta* leaf and looking out at the sunset like a man deeply engrossed in a silent movie. Perfecto appeared before him with his limp little girl in his arms. He was drunk and gaunt and Arnaldo knew right away it killed Perfecto to have to appeal to him. But Arnaldo, the nobody he disdained, had now become his only hope.

"You look like a man who's thinking of trading his soul to the devil, cousin Perfecto."

Perfecto didn't answer. He just stood there, listing like a sinking ship, proffering his daughter, holding her at arm's length, silent tears from his blue Canary-Island eyes streaming down his stubby face, staring at Arnaldo the way a motorist on a one-lane highway looks at an oncoming truck.

Arnaldo rose slowly from his rocking chair, more like an elder shaman than the seventeen-year-old boy he was, and held the girl in his arms, pressing her firmly against his heart.

"If I by Beelzebub cast out devils, by whom do your children cast them out?" he said in English, in the King James version.

Perfecto understood this to be an incantation, a strange speaking-in-tongues that his cousin was performing. He closed his eyes and knelt down on the red-dirt road, knelt down at nothing in particular because he had no faith in any deity or Catholic saint, although at this moment, and from that moment on, he had a fearful faith in his first cousin Arnaldo.

It came to Arnaldo to recite the Beatitudes while he stood there with his first cousin's child in his arms, wondering what Jesus would have done next. When he got to "Blessed are the pure in heart for they shall see God," he suddenly saw a waterfall of green neon fish burst over his head and splatter like a giant egg on a greasy pan. He felt the coolness of the water bathing him and little Ermenegilda. He felt it thoroughly soaking his toes, his tongue and his penis. Later he described the feeling to himself like that of water suddenly turned into light, and found a parallel between that and the turning of water into wine.

He looked at Ermenegilda's eyes, and instead of colors or eyelids or pupils he saw monarch butterflies rising from her skull to hover about her head like a shimmering halo. Her mouth was the fresh flesh of the *mamey* fruit; her skin was a cluster of cut diamonds.

"She's crying! She's crying! Let her go! Release her, you monster!" Arnaldo heard Perfecto scream.

He placed the child in her father's arms once again and, without so much as an eyedropper of emotion in his voice, said in a strange, archaic Spanish: "This damsel is not dead but sleepeth. She will minister to you in the morning."

The next day, before the backyard rooster woke Perfecto, someone saw little Ermenegilda dressed in her satin party dress and her torn patent leather shoes, feeding the chickens and singing the revolutionary anthem—*Venceremos*, we shall win—which one of the bearded rebels who had come down from the Sierra Maestra looking for rice, sugar and coffee had taught her on the day she had come down with polio.

From then on, Arnaldo's life changed at the mill. His *compañeros* insisted that he work only half days and spend the rest of the time tending to his "other world": reading the books, praying in his tongues, and performing an occasional miracle when one was needed. Each bracero gave him ten *centavos* a day from his own wages, and each man contributed a gift in honor of his talents.

Perfecto built Arnaldo a terra-cotta floor, and the foreman, who had treated him like a mangy dog since he started working in the mill at age six, built a whole new wing on the back of Arnaldo's hut where he could receive the faithful, who came not only for miracles but to ask his advice or simply to sit downwind of his breath and look into the eyes of a living holy man.

Word of his first miracle had spread like wild-fire, and people told Arnaldo they had even heard about his powers in Havana. Arnaldo corrected them each time, reminding them that the powers were not his but His that sent him, and he refused to discuss his cures, which grew by the week from healing more polio cases to removing a wart and a birthmark from the foreman's sister that had spread like a bat's wing along the left side of her face.

Finally, the news and proofs of his miracles reached within the walls of the Ona residence, *la Casa Grande*—a nineteenth-century Spanish lime-stone mansion with marble halls and Doric columns and crystal chandeliers so magnificent that they looked like stars and moons and distant planets to Arnaldo when, as a child, he watched from the ser-vant's quarters and waited for the million yellow lights to burst through the French windows in the night.

They came at exactly three in the morning: the Spanish butler, the black cook of Nigerian ancestry, and Don Mario Ona himself, wearing his Panama hat and starchy *guayabera* as though this were the middle of the day and he were deciding how many tons of sacked and sewn sugar to sell the United Fruit Company. But his face didn't look like the middle of the day to Arnaldo. It looked like the face of a man at sea who's just watched a monster rise from the deep and chew his baby daughter alive, spindly legs and tiny chest with little gold medals of Saint Barbara, Baby Jesus, Sacred Heart and all.

"They say you can help... Can you help me? Can you help my wife? Can you bring back my Patricia, our daughter, our only daughter, our precious..."

Patricia's image filled the room. Haughty Patricia, who at seventeen was almost as tall as he, with horse-mane hair down to her waist in a ponytail and emerald eyes that looked so much like the sea that once when his eyes met hers, Arnaldo imagined he'd seen fish and bright points of single-cell amoebas.

Her soul was departing. He knew this not just because Don Mario would have certainly exhausted every other means before calling on him, Arnaldo, the lowest scum in his mill, but because he felt Jesus right there in his hut beside him, raising Lazarus from the dead, saying in King James English, "Patricia, take up thy bed and walk."

Once in the Ona mansion, Arnaldo tried not to look around the girl's bedroom or even notice the fine Spanish-lace pillows and petit-point bedspread where she lay dead under the gossamer mosquito netting. His eyes covered the beautiful young woman. Her round, thick lips were purple cold, and her wide green eyes were transfixed, glued and lifeless like desiccated grasshoppers clinging to the damask knot on the four-poster bed.

Arnaldo felt the night breeze come in through the mahogany shutters that looked down on the mill and on his thatched-roof hut where the oil lamp had been left burning on his books.

He began reciting The Lord's Prayer to himself, but the mother's laments broke his concentration. She made desperate sounds, like the squeals of squirrels or small fowl when he wrung their necks or put a knife or stake to their soft muscle.

He turned to her and to Don Mario and the three attending servants, and in the distant tone that came over him whenever he was given the task of miracles, he said, "Leave me alone with her," remembering the way Jesus had put everyone out of the room when he brought the damsel forth.

The weeping mother was reluctant, fearful that Arnaldo, if left alone, would perform some strange act of African *santería* on her dead daughter, gouge out her heart or her beautiful eyes, suck them out of their sockets, and roll them like marbles under his tongue.

"I am not come to destroy, but to fulfill," he said. And although the words of themselves had no meaning to the poor squealing mother or the grief-stricken *hacendado* in his Panama hat, they left the room obediently and shut the door behind them.

But once alone with her, a powerful want such as he had never known came over Arnaldo.

At that moment, alone with Patricia who slept the sleep of death on the rich, imported Spanish sheets, the gossamer netting hanging overhead, Arnaldo was overcome with ravenous desire to enter the young woman, to possess her not only with his enormous erect member, but with his hands and teeth and famished heart. He threw himself at her side and, suspending her above him with both arms, pried her lifeless legs open with his knees and came inside her with a sharp wild cry.

Don Mario Ona and his wife burst into the room, frightened by the animal cry, thinking that Arnaldo had indeed performed African voodoo and killed their daughter a second time. But what their eyes were allowed to see was simply the young couple propped up on the bed, fully dressed, looking peacefully into space.

Patricia appeared not like a child who had just pried herself from the gnarled claws of death, but like a bride glowing at the altar of love. Arnaldo was composed, alert and quiet, as behooved a young *campesino* who, although a miracle worker, remained mindful of his place.

The grateful parents—his *dueños*, owners, for all intents and purposes—asked Arnaldo to stay and live with them in the Casa Grande. Don Mario offered him money, anything Arnaldo desired, including schooling at the University of Havana if that were his wish.

But Arnaldo insisted on going back to his hut that early morning and continuing his life as before. He told Don Mario that the Lord had called him to minister only in Oriente province for the time being, and to live humbly among his people.

For fear of betraying their bond, he did not look into Patricia's large green eyes when he left the room.

And he did not know if in fact the Lord wanted him to stay in his hut and live among his people. But he knew he needed to sort out what love had done to him and to go over and over in his mind, in the most minute detail, the miracle that the Lord Jesus had wrought in his loins.

All that morning and for the rest of the day, he sat up, staring at the wall where he had hung a sepia picture of his dead grandmother, her lips and eyes colored in pink. He ran his fingers over the brittle pages of his missionary Bible like a blindman reading braille, feeling Patricia's breath and hair and supple body on his flesh, believing himself still inside her, believing that Amazing Grace had visited him, Arnaldo Saavedra, that early morning in Cuba, in the province of Oriente, at the Ingenio Ona.

 **Two**

Despite believing Jesus had told him in his sleep that she would, Patricia did not come to visit him that second early morning. But he waited patiently, knowing that a man's time is not God's time and that, with the Lord, one day is as a thousand years.

He went about the business of preparing the bridal chamber and, mindful of the story of the foolish virgins, put aside extra oil for his lamp. He dreamed of lying with her naked in his arms, of seeing her, every inch of her, like an icon to be worshiped with one's eyes as well as with one's hands and mouth.

At first, Arnaldo could not imagine what conversation Patricia could possibly entertain with a lowly peasant like him. But he felt the Lord, if He discerned his thought, would scold him as He did poor stuttering Moses and say, *who made thy mouth*, and command his speech with the thunder of Sinai.

When Patricia arrived on the third day, it was late, later than he believed was safe for her to sneak from her bed and still be back in time to receive the servants in her room who brought the sweet cream and French pastries he imagined the whole Ona family consumed while he and the rest of the *campesinos* were drinking their coffee with sugar and their sugar with coffee to muster energy and give themselves to the land.

Patricia wore a simple white dress, closed down the front with mother-of-pearl buttons. Her ponytail had been loosened and spread around her shoulders like a shawl. Arnaldo felt her coming— although no one could have heard her because she wore cloth sandals and trod as lightly as an angel. Her emerald eyes lit his hut, and he understood that in the presence of such light the lamps would be unnecessary.

They spent two short hours under the covers his grandmother had sewn together with patches of dresses his mother wore back in 1945. Arnaldo kissed every inch of her, as he had dreamed, lingering on the soles of her feet, her thighs, her stomach, devouring her sweet essence. Patricia was easy in his arms, responding to his skillful manly thrusts as openly and gently as she did to his howling and barking and to his boyish tears which he could not contain each time he entered her.

From then on, night after night for three full moons, their trysts were spent in the rapture and wonder of their bodies.

Once, she told him a story about her trip to Havana, where they made fun of people from the provinces and men wore their Sunday white drill suits every day of the week. She worried about her parents discovering her empty bed in the middle of the night. She longed to be free of them, to leave the *ingenio* and Cuba altogether and go with him to *el norte*, perhaps Miami or Key West, where they could learn about the planets, the forests, the oceans and the rivers that comprise the mysterious universe.

He told her his favorite Bible stories, substituting the key names for Arnaldo and Patricia. So that, for example, in the story of Ruth, Arnaldo turned out to be ninety and Patricia a young Moabite who gleaned the cane fields for him.

These stories seemed to equalize the class differences between them, since he almost always was the hero and she the faithful maid. On any given night, she was Mary Magdalene anointing his feet, Martha ministering to the disciples, Sarah bearing him children, Queen Esther sacrificing her throne.

He came to believe there really was no Big House or Little House between them, no *campesino* and no lady of the house. There was only them, Arnaldo and Patricia, the young lovers whom God

27

had appointed for a purpose—a purpose that, blessed assurance, would be revealed in time.

He felt it before she told him, the swelling in her belly, kicking and tossing wildly and growing stronger each night against the thrusts of his ravenous member. Soon there was nothing to hide. At three months she looked like nine and long overdue. Don Mario Ona did not wait to be told and was not slow to figure out who the father was. Arnaldo, that scum, that orphan boy, that witch who saved his precious daughter's life only to dishonor her and him, Don Mario, Oriente's most feared and honored *hacendado*.

For Don Mario and his wife and all the servants that surrounded them, this pregnancy was clearly an act of the devil and possibly a conspiracy concocted by Castro's slugs to bring down the last vestige of human decency in the province. And this being the case, Don Mario had to face it *como todo un hombre*—that is to say, like a *macho*.

"You will leave the country for any other country in this hemisphere and never again attempt to contact her in any way. As it is, you may not see her ever again, nor see the child she bears. In exchange you will have $1,000 to start life over with. As you can see, I am a generous man. I could have President Batista throw you in jail and let you rot among the gutter rats for the rest of your worthless life, you scum."

But Don Mario did not count on Arnaldo's powers of discernment or his ability to sometimes read an adversary's thoughts as clearly as a man watching John Wayne on a movie screen.

Arnaldo saw Don Mario's real intentions—to hang him from a *ceiba* tree that very night and later take his sweet Patricia and their holy child somewhere to *el norte*. There, neither gossip nor the rebels could get to him or to the thousands of American dollars he planned to stuff in his *guayabera*.

Arnaldo decided to make plans of his own, to abduct Patricia from the Casa Grande, even if it meant leaving on a leaky boat like Peter the fisherman, thinking that Jesus could show him how to walk on water, too, if it became absolutely necessary.

He bit his lip like a lowly peasant and bowed before Don Mario, slumping his shoulders, walking away without turning his back, taking both their secrets with him.

But it was December 31, 1959, and more was happening in Cuba than Arnaldo's sad love story. The following day, President Batista was to flee Cuba and Fidel Castro was to start his slow descent from the mountains to the capital where the multitude was waiting to embrace him and crown him and throw itself at his Jeep.

Arnaldo had taken his books, his grandmother's picture, the clothes on his back and the makeshift quilt where he and Patricia had traded hearts. He had headed for the foothills of the Sierra Maestra, near the rebel barracks, hoping for shelter until the time came when, believing he was long gone, Don Mario would let down his guard. Then Arnaldo would scale the walls of the Casa Grande, burst through the window, and like a mighty Samson, take Patricia in his arms.

But as it happened, back in 1959, at the starting line of that bloody Revolution, rockets glared and bullets were fired by loyalists, by peasants, by *hacendados*, by children and grown men, and no one knew whose side anyone was on or what store or house or mill to loot or ransack first. And, as his twisted destiny would have it, Arnaldo was wounded twice—once by a Castro guerrilla who mistook him for a mercenary, and then by an ex-policeman who saw him licking a pot of rice with a rebel on the very first night he had run for his life.

And so, what might have taken weeks took months—five months, to be exact. Because the second time Arnaldo nearly bled to death and was found unconscious by a six-year-old orphan boy named Mejoral, after the brand name of Cuban aspirins. The boy fed him caterpillars and yuca roots and hid him in a hut made of *ceiba* branches and *guano* leaves and nursed him until he was finally able to speak and remember his name. In running from village to village in this civil war, and slicing his right toe in half and puncturing both ears in the process, Arnaldo lost the books the orange-haired missionary had given him along with his grandmother's picture and his mother's quilt.

Five months after the coming of the Revolution, wounded and without his sacred books, he no longer looked like the young man who'd blossomed like a mutant butterfly. His skin was more like green bananas than golden mangos and his voice could not be heard resonating in the air. But he had recovered his strength and his dream had never left him. With his last breath, he would have crawled and scratched his way to Patricia and his baby.

As soon as he remembered his own name and could walk a straight line without fainting from the punctured ears and the sudden dizzy spells, he began his journey back to the Plantation Ona.

"My child must be born by now," he said to Mejoral. Was it a boy or a girl? He asked Jesus to tell him so he could pick a name. A hundred times over he cried out like Samuel, *Speak, Oh Lord, Thy Servant Heareth*. But Jesus refused to say.

He reached the Casa Grande at three in the morning, at the same hour he had once, many months before, seen Patricia lifeless under the gossamer netting. And this time, on May 13, 1959, after stealing his way through the cane fields and the marble halls and the chandelier stairs like a barefoot phantom, he found his lover's body hard and purple cold once again. He stood shaking and weeping by the door, watching the doctor and the nurse and Don Mario Ona with his wife, hearing words he could never forget: "She has left us." He watched the doctor slide her green eyes shut with his large hairy thumb and the nurse smother her face with a lace *mantilla*.

He meant to scream and rent the room apart. He meant to throw himself on his knees and ask Jesus for a miracle, just one last miracle and no more. But he was overcome by a large frozen dagger that entered his head from the ceiling and pinned him by the pit of his stomach. It was Michael the Archangel, telling him his Patricia was gone, and gone this time forever. Then, suddenly, miraculously, in the dark, he heard a child cry. He could not measure the speed of his steps nor how he hid her in his shirt, covering her wails with his mouth, nor how he found his way three miles outside of the Ona compound without leaving a trace.

His daughter had just been born that day. And like the poet José Martí's beloved, Patricia was the girl from Oriente province who had died for love.

He would have called her Patricia, but the name Esmeralda—for her emerald eyes, luminous and identical to her mother's—came to him as if Patricia had whispered it.

"Esmeralda you are," he said, and he took his daughter to the orphan boy who had saved his life, and together they stole a clam boat with an outboard motor, pried the anchor from the rocks and the seaweed mounds, and sailed for *el norte*, not knowing exactly where that was, but sure that the Ona dogs would find them if they didn't run first.

At the Ingenio Ona, another orphan child was crying in Don Mario Ona's arms. They named him Juan. He had large eyes, mystical and green and captivating like those of his twin sister.

Three

Esmeralda had heard the story of her birth and rescue at least once a month. It was part of a ritual that was somehow tied to the spiders, caterpillars and winged cockroaches that crawled on her during her father's apparitions.

As far as she finally remembered, it had started when she was four and they were living on One Hundred and Seventeenth Street, in a turn-of-the-century Manhattan tenement house, in a railroad apartment with iron bars on the windows to keep the night thieves out.

Arnaldo was a changed man since the perilous trip on the high seas with his newborn baby in his arms and the orphan boy Mejoral at the mast. If someone had told Esmeralda how her father looked as a boy of sixteen when he was born-again and then at seventeen when he had met and loved her mother, she would have thought it was one more Cuban fable.

The man Esmeralda knew was a sad and tired *guajiro*, a peasant who had vomited the ways of his new country like bitter medicine, a young man who had grafted on his skin and on his melancholy eyes the death sentence of old men. In those days, back on One Hundred and Seventeenth Street, Esmeralda slept in the living room on a sofa bed, and Arnaldo slept on a cot in the kitchen, which was open and right next to the living room and the sofa bed. It was a dreary apartment, freezing in winter because the steam never made its way as far up as the fourth floor and sweltering in summer because they had no air conditioning.

Years later, she still remembered the smell of burnt sugar and splattering lard from the Puerto Rican *cuchifrito* store on the first floor, how it wafted up to her bed and made her stomach rumble in the middle of the night. She would stare at the refrigerator from her bed, but keep still, holding her breath, scared to reach for milk, afraid to wake her father and bring on his apparitions.

But they came anyway, sure as snow in February, sure as the jeers of the young Puerto Rican boys who followed her down the street pulling on their budding testicles while making obscene gestures at Esmeralda's invincible beauty. These apparitions had the face of a man moving in a dream, of a desperate deep-sea diver screaming through glass. Sometimes she was awake when he came, as if expecting the inevitable. Earlier, when she was four and five, his voice would rouse her like a fire alarm. It was always the same, a liturgical ritual, a droning and lamenting like the prayers of a Muslim at sunrise.

"Are you awake, Esmeralda?" he would say. And, no matter what she answered or even if she pretended not to hear, he would go on: "Your father wants to tell you a story before it's too late and we're seized up in the Heavenly Rapture."

He would slip naked in her bed, draw her near, and tell his tale of how he healed the little girl of polio or the grown man of measles. He'd speak of her mother, of her beauty and how she died of love. He'd mention his long and painful trip to Key West with her in his arms and then confess he had done unspeakable things to save her life. But he would never say what.

And while he told his stories in his slow, hypnotic voice, his wide, rough hands caressed her throat, her rosebud breasts, her girlish arms. He would slip his fingers between her thighs and prod her petals with his thumb. He would press his hungry member against her, forcing himself only slightly, mindful of not rupturing the virgin swath, letting his hot, viscous explosion run down her like a waterfall.

Esmeralda breathed frantically at his side, begging for air, feeling engulfed in nests of bat-winged roaches and giant spiders. Each time, she froze with fear so black that long after he had gone back to his cot, she would still be lying there in rigor mortis, unable to move a toe or shut her eyelids.

But that was her night-father. Her day-father was a simple, kindly man who had difficulty speaking English, except when he quoted from the King James Bible, who worked as a janitor and served as a minister of his own church. Well, not a church, a congregation he called church and which met at a Hispanic social club, Hot Mambo, early on Sunday mornings when the regular members were home sleeping off the Saturday night liquor, the dance, and tobacco smoke.

For years, there were two fathers and two lives for Esmeralda, and neither one spoke to the other or knew whether the other was real or imagined.

By age twelve, she was fully grown and had blossomed—a ravishing young virgin with seafaring eyes, chestnut hair down to her shoulders, and lips and cheeks and a high waist that reminded her teachers at PS 155 of Rita Hayworth during her *Gilda* years. She seemed to have natural style, so that her jeans and sweat shirts and simple cotton dresses took on a special *je ne sais quoi*. That's what her French teacher, Mrs. Goldburg, called it, meaning style, a style that seemed inbred but which was quite above her provenance, at least the one anyone knew anything about.

Esmeralda was good in school, especially good at English and history and anything that involved speaking in tongues. Human tongues, that is, for she disdained the other and was not yet aware of her own magical gifts. She got the lead part in the school play twice—*Annie* and *Annie Get Your Gun*—although her singing was not as good as Moira Flaherty, who sang like an angel but didn't have Esmeralda's stage presence or blind devotion from her fellow students. And that surprised Esmeralda, who didn't feel at all on the inside like she seemed to the world on the outside. She felt scared, too scared to really be connected to mundane things like plays or school or friends at PS 155. What she accomplished, she thought she did by imitation, or maybe thanks to a sixth sense that ran her life on automatic pilot. There was always a little tremor going on inside her, like the rumble of the Lexington Avenue subway rattling the grids on the street. She was the street, and her fear was the train, running on her tracks anytime it pleased.

And then there was the immense pity she called love, or the unquantifiable love she called pity, that she felt for her father Arnaldo. So that, no matter how long her cockroach and batwing nights were or how scared she felt in school during the day, Esmeralda wanted above all things to please her father and restore to him the happiness he had once felt back in Cuba under the coconut trees, when he was the living patron saint of his village and her mother made him feel like a man, *todo un hombre*—who, because of her love, was as tall and powerful as the most *hacendado hacendado* in the whole of Oriente province.

One evening in November, at age seventeen, when the railroad apartment on One Hundred and Seventeenth Street had started to gather the knife-blade chill around the seams and mouse holes and unevenly plastered walls that would numb her olive skin by late December, Esmeralda made a discovery that was to seal forever that unquantifiable love and enormous pity she felt for her poor immigrant father. It was a dark discovery that was revealed quite naturally with the flat-line tones of the man at the information booth in Grand Central Station reading the train schedules off the board.

And in Esmeralda that revelation, because of who she was and how she had grown up—her soul tilting on the emotional hemp hammock her father had cradled her in since birth—awakened a feeling unlike what another young woman her age living in New York that year might have felt.

This was a knowledge that could have hurled her away from Arnaldo in a stampede of revulsion, perhaps propelled her once and for all into the sacred crypt and mores of the North American, Anglo-Saxon culture that was the bedrock beneath the hard silver rocks in Central Park and supported everything she had ever learned at PS 155 and Julia Richman High School. But instead, her father's confession opened wide the doors of Esmeralda's heart, drawing father and daughter closer under the satin cape of some ancestral *matador*, sealing in her a deep desire to do everything within her power to make things right for Arnaldo once again and restore the years that the locust had eaten.

That evening in November when Esmeralda came home, Arnaldo was stretched out on her sofa bed listening to Radio WADO, the Puerto Rican station that played cha-cha and salsa and other music he hated, but which also brought news about Latin America and very often news about Cuba. He always wanted to know what was going on in Cuba, what Fidel Castro was up to, how the Russians were treating him, and how the sugar crop in Oriente province was doing now that the U.S. had managed a total blockade. He was never interested in politics per se, because to him politics were worldly things, things that belonged to Roman emperors and Pharisees and not to the heirs of the Lord Jesus. And he never called himself an "exile" the way the Cubans in Miami and the Upper East Side did. He called himself a Cuban-to-the-bone. And only jokingly did he call Esmeralda an American, because, as he told her, "What I am, you are, and that's not what I am." Before the revelation that evening, she used to say, "I may have been Cuban once for five minutes, but

I'm not one now. I grew up here. I live here. English is my language and I have nothing to do with Cuba. We don't even have family there!" And Arnaldo would shake his head. "Did you ever see a mango turn into a banana? Well, when you see that, that's the day you can say you're not Cuban."

Esmeralda made herself a cup of herb tea and settled on a chair, facing her father. "Tell me the story of how you left Cuba," she asked him, as she had asked a thousand times before, always wanting to know more, hoping that as he told the story, she could see her mother's face projected on the wall. For Arnaldo had never had a picture of Patricia, and Esmeralda longed to see what her beautiful and extraordinary face looked like.

And this time Arnaldo told more than he had told before. "The things, the terrible things I did to save your life when I left Cuba, my country and your country, Esmeralda, they are things I don't think any man has ever done."

"What did you do on that boat that was so bad, *papá*?"

"I killed a boy, Esmeralda. I killed a young boy who had saved my life. It was burning in that little clam boat under the sun all day, with nothing but salt water for miles and miles right down to the end of the world—and no boat, and not one American in sight. You were crying, my poor little girl, in my arms. Your sweet wafer lips had blisters on them,

41

and I had just about run out of spit to feed you. I did it before I knew I was doing it. I saw that strong orphan boy standing there. And you, my newborn baby... I could not do this to your mother. Suddenly, I had my hands around the boy's neck. I squeezed and squeezed and felt his nut crack. It was no different than killing a chicken, than killing a squirrel in the fields because you haven't eaten in days and God forgives you. And I pricked his veins with my teeth, Esmeralda, one by one, and fed you from them like a fountain, and wet your blisters till you were firm and whole again. And I fed us both from little tender pieces of his flesh. Little tiny morsels which I chewed for you first. And then your tiny gums sucked on them like mother's milk. Later, a fishing vessel found us. But by then I had turned over what was left of poor Mejoral to the bottom of the sea. Up until now, no one else has known what your first meal was, my little Esmeralda, or how the Lord Jesus communed with us during our sacred supper in those early days."

Esmeralda felt a grip in her heart as painful, she reckoned, as poor Mejoral must have felt gasping for air under the sun, having his neck squeezed like a chicken on that leaky boat, giving up his flesh to save hers. But then, only seconds later, the pain and horror that shook her dove like an eel beneath the sand and sea, the same sea that had engulfed poor Mejoral.

And, suddenly, it was pride and wonder at her father that floated up to the surface like a water lily in Esmeralda's heart. She felt pity for poor Mejoral, but it was the pity she had felt when she had caught the Puerto Rican boys at the tennis courts by the East River plucking the feathers of a sparrow that had been impaled in the chicken-wire fence for days. His soul was gone and there was nothing left to mourn.

The pride and wonder that glowed in her heart for her father, an anointed preacher and a man of God, as he called himself, happened when, upon imagining the scene on that sun-stroked boat frame by frame as someone editing a movie, it came to her that Arnaldo had cared for her so much as to kill a man and risk going to Hell. And then, a moment later, still viewing those frames in slow motion, it dawned on her that Arnaldo had loved her mother so much as to never want another woman again. Esmeralda did not consider Arnaldo's nightly visitations wanting a woman, but rather longing for the one who'd died giving birth to her in Cuba.

And from that November evening on, at seventeen, her father's age when he had met her mother, Esmeralda was immersed in a holy river of forgiveness for her father and for all the times he had come to her naked in the night. It was a wide, deep river, as pure and full of crystal angels as she imagined Jesus had made the River Jordan when He dunked His head.

That evening Esmeralda's fear of her night-father ceased at once, and the subway tremors stopped and the batwing cockroaches faded when next he approached her in the moonlit dark. And there emerged in place of all the years of fear, a world of wonder where every night she saw herself floating on a bed of rainbow-colored butterflies, hovering over sky and sea, free and cleansed by the salt air, swaddled in a soft honeysuckle breeze.

This sudden inversion, this turning of her universe inside out from a new lighthouse, became the first foretelling in Esmeralda's heart that life, as her father had preached a thousand times, was not made entirely of things which do appear. And with that thought came hope in the evidence of things not seen, hope that someday her mother Patricia would manifest herself before them in the living room at One Hundred and Seventeenth Street, and that Arnaldo would be a happy man once again, with golden skin the color of ripe mangos and a smile so wide that even the sad pigeons by the school yard would sing.

Four

There was a story about Cuban women—well, not a story, but a way of classifying them—which Esmeralda had heard Arnaldo tell. It divided women into three categories: Bananas, Mangos and Coconuts.

Bananas are the tall, thin ones: self-contained one-piece suits without curves to hang on to or blue grottos to navigate. You have to peel them back to eat them, and sometimes they are too green and sometimes too ripe. In either case, it's often hard to tell what you will get beforehand.

Mangos are the best kind because they are sweet and their skin is so thin you can prick it with your front teeth and let the juice run freely in your mouth. Mangos are firm and full of promise. They release all the fragrance of God's dewy earth as soon as you pluck them from the tree and float them on the palm of your hand.

Coconuts, on the other hand, are also good. Coconut women are the ones with round firm breasts that have never nursed and consequently tremble with milk inside. Coconut women are hard to crack because they tend to be reserved. And, like the fruit, they fall in two distinct categories: the green ones, which are the ones swelling with thick clear milk; and the brown ones, which have no milk but nurse such cool silvery flesh, painted the color of the moon, that even the blade of a dull *machete* can melt their hearts with a single blow.

That November, in her seventeenth year, Esmeralda, who had always classified herself as a banana in spite of her pomegranate mouth and her cinnamon-toast skin that smelled of jasmine in the wind and her invincible wide and green seafaring eyes that captivated even strangers in the street, began to think of herself as a green coconut.

And although this new level, which also coincided with her graduation from Julia Richman High School, may have seemed more in keeping with who she was, it was not the way she was seen by her few acquaintances and the rest of her world between One Hundred and Seventeenth Street and Sixty Eighth Street. She had no friends in the ordinary way that girls her age have friends. At seventeen, just before her vision and her life began to turn, Esmeralda still saw herself as an invisible observer in a world of adults, incapable of making ripples in her path or of awakening her own heart to the kind of romantic love Arnaldo felt for Patricia, or even the kind of infatuation she heard Julio Iglesias and Olga Guillot sing about. There were young men and men twice her age who looked on her with admiration, and women who loved women whom fate brought to her door with enormous regularity and then suddenly were plucked from her life before she ever truly understood what their want meant.

This bringing and then plucking of people from her life seemed to take an almost identical course each time. It happened, for example, with Rob Sanders, her high school English teacher. He was a pale man, thirty years old, whose passion before encountering Esmeralda had been the literary dissection of Molly Bloom's passage in *Ulysses*. He was a man who from the start taught the whole class of seniors looking only into Esmeralda's eyes. It also happened when Esmeralda took a job, her first real job other than waiting tables at a greasy spoon on Ninety-Sixth Street, as a receptionist at a beauty salon on Seventy-Sixth and Madison.

At school, she met Rob Sanders and, he said, the first day of class he fell in love with her. At the beauty salon, making appointments, adding up cutting and coloring and perming bills and calling up to check on people's credit cards, she met a client, a famous woman of 40, a Broadway star who invited her for high tea at the Carlyle Hotel. The famous woman also fell in love with her, she said, at first sight. The woman called herself Cristina, but told her it was her given name and not her stage name, which anyone, even Esmeralda, might recognize. Esmeralda had remembered seeing her face on a poster or a magazine. But she had never been to a Broadway show because Arnaldo said they were, for the most part, the work of the Devil.

Neither of these suitors—nor the others who came and left like dreamers made pale and confused by an unsettling discovery—would be of any significance to the story of Arnaldo and Esmeralda and Juan and how their fates were twisted in a tragic path, except to point to the girl and then to the woman Esmeralda was and the one she eventually became.

While others were looking at Esmeralda like a luscious mango they wanted to devour, a rare Rita Hayworth beauty they longed to consume for no other reason than her disturbing sensuality and elegance, Esmeralda was still wrapped in her cocoon. She had not yet awakened to the meaning of love, lust or desire, except when it came to her love and pity of her father, her hope for her mother's resurrection, and her night and day dreams which, by seventeen, had already begun to exert their pull on her from their hidden reality. Although she was an A student, particularly when it came to languages and the humanities, and although she seemed mature in the brief conversations she had with strangers, what those who attempted to possess her found when they looked deep was a child of perhaps nine or ten who carried secret conversations with imaginary lizards she called by their surnames and butterflies that she said she often accompanied on their flights to Miami, Cuba and further down to Nicaragua, Ecuador and the Brazilian Rain Forest. She favored particularly the Ghost butterfly, with its transparent body and eyes on the tips of its wings, and the blue Morpho butterfly, which she said gave off a special iridescent light that enabled her to see through solid bodies from the sky.

None of this truth came out until those who approached her for the purpose of consuming her mango fruit opened their hearts to her in their particular brand of sophisticated intimacy. It was mostly the sophisticated who dared approach Esmeralda; the simple looked at her from afar or called out to her in the street in obscene jeers, but seemed to intuit in her a frightful singularity that kept them at bay, as a tiger or a monstrous spotted salamander might make someone stare and then recoil.

After months of burning for her at night and on weekends, Rob Sanders holed up in his pack-rat apartment and wrote odes to Esmeralda's beauty which he submitted to *The New Yorker* and *Ploughshares* and other magazines of literary bent (only to receive almost immediate rejection slips). Finally, he mustered the courage to ask Esmeralda out for dinner one evening.

Esmeralda liked him. She was fascinated by his pale skin, the pasty color of cream crayons, and by his reddish freckled hands, which reminded her of a butterfly she had seen pinned to a tropical drawing on the first floor of the Museum of Natural History. When he asked her to join him alone, she knew instinctively that it was meant as a secret act between them and that she would not be able to share it with her father or her schoolmates. But she did not know exactly what that secret act meant or why a big teacher like Sanders would want to spend time with her. Mostly, she went with him because he favored her and because she had not yet, at seventeen, learned to say no to people her father's age. She had no idea what it was like to like someone, really like someone, in the manner that Rob Sanders thought of her, or what to do if he should offer himself in the way Arnaldo did during his nightly apparitions.

After dinner and then an ice cream soda at Peppermint Park, after the conversation where Mr. Sanders—she called him that before that day and even after, in spite of what happened—did most of the talking, Esmeralda found herself in his small studio. She made room on his sofa between the books and typewritten manuscripts piled up in little hills against the wall and stared at the paperbacks in his efficiency kitchen and stacked up on the electric burners where she guessed immediately he had never even boiled an egg.

Rob Sanders lay on the floor at her feet while she sat up between two rows of books on each side of the frayed chintz couch. He drank Irish whiskey, which he kept as a relic from his last bicycle tour of Ireland, and offered Esmeralda a Coke. Esmeralda noticed he did not smoke, a fact that pleased her, for she thought of smokers as very nervous people with grimy and smelly tongues. She sat still, her plain white cotton dress over her knees and her legs crossed. She felt uncomfortable at first making contact with his brown eyes, although she was used to their stare by now. It was different to have Mr. Sanders look at her in a classroom full of students than alone in his strange, bookish apartment. And it was different to sit in front of him and be expected to carry on a conversation than to just listen and answer an occasional question she had looked up the night before.

He told her about his childhood on Long Island, and how he loved baseball and almost made it to the big leagues like Carl Yastrzemski, also a Long Island boy. He then described his studies at some big university in Dublin where he had majored in James Joyce, then spoke of his marriage and divorce from someone who it seemed to Esmeralda had been a very cold, cruel woman his own age. He also told her about his nervous breakdown, his hellish sojourn at the Paine Whitney Clinic, and his job as a teacher at Julia Richman High School, two blocks away from the hospital where only five years before he had been forced to walk around in paper slippers.

He seemed to rush his story, wanting to bare his soul all in one swoop, needing Esmeralda and Esmeralda's eyes to cast a healing balm over his life. All through his monologue, he sat up on the floor holding his knees up with his freckled hands, looking deep into her eyes with a long and melancholy searchlight.

And Esmeralda felt a certain closeness to him. But it wasn't the closeness of a woman for a man, but rather the marvel of the lepidopterist examining the new catch in her net. Although at that point it was not clear who was the prey. Was it the innocent and ravishing seventeen-year-old Cuban-American girl who had been so shell-shocked by the ancient and rural ways of her father as to be entirely out of reach of the mating games of those living in Manhattan at the end of the twentieth century? Or was it the once-professor and Joycean scholar and now public high school teacher of inner city children who, quoting Yeats, told her how all day long he looked upon her beauty and felt like "a marble triton among the streams?" The Yeats' quote was a phrase Esmeralda liked, although she did not understand the meaning. She had to wait to get home that evening to look up the word *triton* in the dictionary.

Once he arrived at his inevitable confession and told her how he longed for her beauty and how he felt like a triton in the streams, Rob Sanders had no other recourse but to leap for his prey and press his mouth and legs upon her.

With that act, he burst out in tears of sexual desperation. And Esmeralda, rather than recoiling or displaying fear, simply watched him without participating in his folly. He kissed her and she kept her pomegranate lips sealed tight like a tamarind pod. And her eyes opened, staring at him fixedly in microscopic proximity.

No matter how much his passion advanced, Esmeralda remained poised, waiting for the storm to pass or the volcano to erupt and melt away, the way she had done with her father, the way she was accustomed to receiving a man.

And Rob Sanders, overcome by her icy stillness and perfected remoteness, and not knowing how to interpret the signs (for he had been rejected before, but forcefully or furiously or gently or verbally), began feeling how Esmeralda had felt as a child growing up in East Harlem, unheard, unfelt, unable to speak or make a ripple in life. In short, he began to think of himself as a man whose identity and presence in the world was rapidly disappearing.

He pulled away and attempted to hide his humiliation by smoothing his red hair and cupping his eyes in his hands. And Esmeralda, freed of the burden of his heaving frame and his begging heart, felt moved to pat his speckled butterfly hands with her fingers and to share with him her secret life, her communion with lizards and butterflies and her ideas of space travel in the unseen world.

"I'd like to tell you about my friend, Ramira Mendoza," she said, this time peeling his hands away from his eyes, looking at him as the friend she'd hoped he'd be.

"Who is she?" he asked, attempting to compose himself, thinking she was giving him the cue to act civilized and forget the whole incident. "A friend of yours at school?"

"You could say that," Esmeralda answered. "But she's a lizard friend, and she does visit me at school. She goes in places neither of us could fit. She sleeps on leaves and feeds on invisible flies with her tongue. And she pops up suddenly when I least expect her and sings a Cuban song my mother taught her."

Rob Sanders looked up at her, startled, wondering whether Esmeralda was speaking in riddles, trying to send him a message.

"Is that so?" he said, begging for time, dropping his line to the bottom of the lake. "And who else comes to visit you?" By now he had gained a certain distance from the young woman whose beauty had so disturbed his wakeful nights.

"Well, if you really want to know, I can tell you my real friends are actually the butterflies. Mostly the Ghosts and the Morpho butterflies, if you know anything about butterflies. And I am able to travel with them where they go. At night, of course, after my father's gone to sleep. They just take me up on their cloud and we go. Places like Ecuador and down the Orinoco River and the Mato Grosso and well into the Amazon. Did you ever read or see a movie about those places? I'm there. I'm there pretty often, even just hours before I come to your class."

Esmeralda was speaking as naturally as a girl recounting her last trip abroad. There was nothing strained about her voice or manner. Rob Sanders understood she was perfectly serious and—not discerning her magic gifts or her ability to travel in time and space—he became extremely anxious in her presence and, now that his ardor had boomeranged in his face, he wanted nothing more than to see Esmeralda disappear down the hall.

After that day, Rob Sanders looked but once more into Esmeralda's eyes when he taught his class. He did so in an attempt to reconcile the beauty he had seen and died for to the girl who believed she traveled on butterfly wings and who had turned to marble when his skin touched hers.

The Broadway star who called herself Cristina met the same fate in Esmeralda's eyes. Although she did not weep like a fool or throw herself in Esmeralda's arms like the teacher, she brought gifts Esmeralda said her father would not let her accept and grasped a hand that suddenly went limp and stared misty-eyed into her sea-green eyes, only to find a stone as brilliant and as hard as the emerald itself. And when she traced Esmeralda's lips with her finger tips, and when she attempted to fall upon her mouth with a kiss, she, too, found a statue and behind it a girl who was absent and hovering in space like the spirit of those recently departed.

The Broadway star changed hairdressers and Esmeralda never saw her again, except for the dozen times she flashed before her on TV in a commercial for spaghetti sauce.

And while both incidents caused Esmeralda a momentary sadness, she did not blame herself for Mr. Sander's or for Cristina's sudden turn of heart. For by that time, Esmeralda's new life was already beginning to gather speed. She was waking to her gifts, gifts that put her so far outside the daily world of the city and its streets and its railroad tracks running over the *Marqueta* on Park Avenue by her dank, cold house and by her father's makeshift church in the Hot Mambo Social Club, that one Sunday morning during church, she whispered in Arnaldo's ear that, like Jesus, she knew now beyond a shadow of a doubt that while she may be *in* this world, she was not *of* it. Her guidance, she knew, came from above and not from beneath—meaning from soaring in the sky with the gentle butterflies and not from listening to Man, whose breath is in his nostrils.

FIVE

There was a saying in Arnaldo's hometown, the one he thought he was waking up in every morning before his fully conscious state told him he was a refugee working as a janitor, cleaning latrines and separating plastic garbage bags for the sanitation men. The saying went like this: "For every south, there is a north, and even though the north may know nothing of the south or the south of the north, they need each other to be what they are." It was a saying that people usually cut short. "Like the south to the north" they would say, since everyone knew what they meant. They used it when referring to fate in a general way, such as there is bad because there is good, or there are rich people because there are poor people, or there are stupid people because there are smart people. No matter what you applied it to, though, whether it was fate or not, it would work as long as it involved duality— blondes because there are brunettes, short because there is tall, obnoxious because there is graceful, greedy because there is generous.

Juan Saavedra Ona, Arnaldo's son and Esmeralda's twin brother, called himself Juan Ona because his grandfather had adopted him at birth and hid from him the fantastic tale of his conception. He'd had a sharp feeling in his heart almost since the day Esmeralda had arrived as an infant in Key West that he existed because there was another—a south or a north to him—who was the exact otherness and yet exact image of himself.

If someone, a detective or a district attorney for instance, were to interrogate him as to when he first became aware of the existence of his other— the way he was interrogated later about Arnaldo and Esmeralda, mercilessly, cruelly, to the point of exhaustion, watching the vomit spout like a geyser from his mouth—he would have said he had always known it, the way he had known he had a perennial five-o'clock shadow and green eyes the brilliant and disturbing color of Brazilian emeralds.

But although this was so, that Juan had always sensed he had a north or a south living in another part of the world, this notion had not gripped his heart to the point of obsession until he and his twin sister turned nineteen under the same stars at different latitudinal parallels.

Before they turned nineteen, Juan's life seemed to be going in an opposite direction, in a direction away from Esmeralda, that is, and therefore on a path where it would seem unlikely they would meet.

A few months after Fidel arrived in the capital, his men began to confiscate every *ingenio* and every little parcel of land that belonged to the ruling class from Pinar del Rio to Oriente Province. Don Mario Ona, who had stuffed his *guayabera* pockets full of American dollars from the United Fruit Company, packed up his little grandson and his wife María and three servants and airlifted them to Miami, to Key Biscayne, to a red-tile Mizner mansion he had bought for himself and his Tropicana Night Club mistress before Carlos Prío Socarrás came to power—in the late forties, that is, since Prío came before Batista who came before Castro.

And so, while Esmeralda was growing up on One Hundred and Seventeenth Street, starring in school plays at PS 155 and being swaddled and fondled in their father's arms, Juan grew up in Miami as part of the Cuban community—they preferred to call themselves exiles. And he grew up in a manner not different from how he would have grown up in Cuba, except that in Miami, because of the culture at large and the language and the other forty-nine states, Juan would eventually find a route, an underground railroad, where he could leave his roots, even his transplanted roots, and work his own way to his north or to his south, whichever Esmeralda was.

For a boy, and then a young man of great privilege and extraordinary looks, Juan was a melancholy type, a poetic soul prone to bouts of depression and solitude that no one, not even his grandmother, whom he called *Mami*, for she was the only mother he knew, could save him from once they would start their whirly-gig in his mind. And these whirly-gigs, these pregnant clouds, these goblins that would overtake him as often as once a month just before he met his fate, would come upon him, it seemed, for no reason at all. And when they came, his relative world where he existed and did the ordinary things humans do, would have to stop.

If he was playing baseball in the junior leagues he'd quit before the dark cloud could betray him. If he was dating a virgin or having an affair with an older woman—as was his preference since he was twelve and his grandfather's mistress in Key Biscayne initiated him by cutting his fly open with a pair of scissors and reaching importunately for his member—he would announce he'd been overtaken by sudden inspiration and shut himself in his bedroom for days at a time, staring at the ceiling with both hands on his chest and consuming large quantities of Coca-Cola and fried plantains.

His grandparents, whom he thought were his parents who had him late in life, right after his sister Patricia had fallen victim to the polio epidemic, were the only people fully aware of his fits of melancholy. But neither one had faith in doctors, nor did they suggest that he seek medical advice for his strange condition. The resurrection of Patricia at the hands of the voodoo man who dishonored her had contributed to his parents' disdain for the medical profession. Don Mario and Doña María only saw the outward symptoms and not Juan's hell each time the unclean spirits seized him. They regarded their grandson's melancholy as an incurable part of his character, as the south that went with the rest of his general north—meaning by his north, his genius as a portrait artist and his skill as a young architect, as well as his movie-star good looks.

If his south was hell to pay, Don Mario Ona had remarked on several occasions when Juan had been found by a servant hiding under the bed, his north more than made up for it.

The part that no one saw was what Juan called the wringing of his soul. He pictured himself like the shirts his grandmother still had the servants scrub and dry by hand and then hang in the walled courtyard so no one could see the washing on the line, which she said was the mark of the immigrant poor in this country.

This wringing of his soul had its own life span, a life span that once begun, Juan could do nothing but surrender to as both spectator and victim.

The first melancholy seizure came at age four, as far back as he could remember. The next occurred at eleven, the year Esmeralda began to menstruate, and from eleven on, several times a year. The black cloud, the fear, and then the tearful grip usually occurred at night, almost always at the same time Arnaldo was slipping naked into Esmeralda's bed up north on One Hundred and Seventeenth Street in East Harlem.

If Juan were to describe his melancholy to the detective or district attorney who questioned him years later about Arnaldo and Esmeralda, he would say that for no particular reason, and sometimes when his life was going great and he had either finished a commissioned portrait or had just taken a beautiful woman to bed, a sudden sadness would bathe his inner lining like a waterfall, like a long river of blood. Suddenly he would be a ghostly chrysalis sucked empty of his butterfly, an abandoned carcass the elephants had mauled and then forgotten by a riverbed.

And following this melancholic overtaking, he would reason he had nothing in particular to live for and would begin rehearsing in his mind the many ways he could extinguish his brief stay on this planet. It was during this stage, this stage of enumerating and depicting the different modes of suicide, that he would hide under the bed, pretending his room was already swept clean of any trace or remembrance of him.

But towards his nineteenth year something happened to Juan that, although it did not turn entirely his melancholy tide, provided a solace, a way station between his north and his south, and helped him to navigate among the living.

To describe what this way station was, it is necessary to first see Juan from the outside in, as the world of Cuban bankers and museum sponsors in Miami perceived him, as the admissions office at Yale saw him, as the famous senator who had commissioned him to do his portrait when he was only seventeen remembered him.

"A fine, tall, hell of an *hombre*" might be the way the senator would have described him, with a firm pat on the back while addressing a crowd. Or "a sportsman with the gift of Velázquez and Goya rolled into one" might have been the way the museum director might have perceived him. His art teacher, who basically had nothing to teach him because Juan had brought his talents with him from who knows where, would have agreed.

But none—not the senator nor the teachers nor the women who surrendered their hearts before he had a chance to ask—would have described him as he saw himself.

The women remembered him for his looks and would have spoken of his tall lean figure, his square jaw, his jet black hair, his hypnotic eyes. The men would have been struck by his virility and would measure themselves against it. But they would never mention it, except to say, of course, that he was one hell of a guy.

The Cubans in Miami would have said he looked more American than Cuban. And no wonder, because he was raised on hamburgers and very little yuca with rice and beans. The Anglos he knew at his private military schools would have said Juan was just a regular guy, disciplined, luckier than most, a talented artist and a devil with women.

But none would have seen him as Juan saw himself during his melancholy fits, or the way he felt the day his eyes captured his north or his south, whichever Esmeralda happened to be.

He'd had inklings of it before, and when he finally met Esmeralda he understood completely. But that first day when he surprised himself in the mirror—only it wasn't himself— he had no idea what it meant.

At first Juan caught a brief glimpse on his way from the bathroom, where he had just thrown up, to his bed, where he'd planned to spend the next few days until the storm passed, if it passed. For while he was in the throes of it, he fervently believed the goblins would never leave. And, suddenly alarmed, he turned back and stood squarely in front of the mirror and examined every inch of his naked self, in horror and then, moments later, in incredulous glee.

For what he saw was not the handsome, well-endowed young man of nineteen with shiny, virile hair running down the length of him and exposing all the more those parts that women dreamed about long after he'd forgotten their names, but rather a pastoral beauty, a young goddess from the equatorial woods, with eyes as green as his and shoulder-length hair as black and shiny as an Arabian mane and small breasts as round and hard as brown coconuts with sweet, silvery flesh. This creature in the mirror, himself, his other hemisphere, looked and moved and assumed the poses he struck. Only she had a Duchess of Alba, Naked Maja smile on her thick pomegranate lips, and, overhead, instead of a dark cloud, there hung a halo comprised entirely of fluttering Ghost and Morpho butterflies.

Juan stood a long time in front of the reflection, wondering if the ghost would dissipate, questioning his sanity, calling himself a *pájaro*, a *maricón*, a queer, a fag, a repressed pervert and a transvestite—for he'd picked up such prejudices in military school and still subscribed to the *macho* view of bugger and buggee. The image in the mirror gradually began to fill every crevasse in his soul. He suddenly pictured himself as the image saw him and as he saw the image, and he then felt Esmeralda's gaze invade his thoughts like a cool, fresh stream seeping through the bones of his bones, dispossessing him and then possessing him completely. And from that moment on, Juan understood who his north, or his south, was (although he still didn't know where she was), and the image of Esmeralda never left him again. Nor did the picture of himself looking like her in the mirror, so that each time he found himself in bed with a woman, he surrendered that woman who lived inside him to the arms of the woman in bed with him.

Although his melancholy did not leave until the day he finally met his fate, Juan found a way to contain it by appearing in front of his full-length mirror as soon as sadness began to overtake him. He called out to Esmeralda—not yet knowing her name—and stood in prayerful attention before her until every last goblin was chased away like a cowardly satyr by the sylvan beauty in the glass before him.

Six

The years between their nineteenth and their twenty-ninth birthdays could be said in retrospect to have been spent in preparation for their meeting. During those years, while Esmeralda still lived and cooked and cleaned and tended to Arnaldo's life, Juan made a name for himself, first in Miami and then on both coasts, as far west as San Francisco and as far north as Boston. Neither one really knew what fate was bringing to the table. There were always two lives—or four lives, if you added Juan and Esmeralda separately—going on for them at the same time. And while these two lives, or four lives, met in their dreams or in the moments behind the mirror or at the gathering of a snow storm or on the day of the great subway derailment, they were also revolving independently around their own moons, worshipping the indecipherable quotients of their beings.

Juan graduated from the Yale School of Architecture and then went back to portrait painting in

Miami, despite the three residential and one commercial projects in Connecticut that made Paul Goldberger refer to him in *The New York Times* as one of the most promising young architects of the day.

No matter what Juan did or how much he excelled at it, melancholy was always his companion and he never, until he met Esmeralda, felt right in his own skin. "I'm either too large or too small for my skin, and in either case I just don't fit anywhere or with anyone," he would say often when he was trying to end an affair he knew he should never have started in the first place.

This feeling of never fitting anywhere, of being malcontent in spite of his privilege and his looks and his artistic gifts, prompted some Cubans in Miami to label him Tristán Tristón, Sadsack, the comic book character in Spanish translation. "Just look at the Marielitos and other poor Cubans in this country who are still parking cars at the Hotel Fountainbleau," they would say, "and give me one good reason why you shouldn't stop feeling sorry for yourself and wipe that sulk off your face."

And it was not only among Cubans that he elicited jealousy and reproach—particularly when he consumed their women like liquorice jelly beans and charged $25,000 per portrait. Other Hispanic groups as well read about him in the paper, saw his picture in *El Diario* or *El Nuevo Herald*, and concluded that his good fortune stemmed from the fact that he passed for white, looked like a movie star, but had a Spanish surname.

All the political concerns and the struggle among Hispanic groups and the notion of racism or haves and have-nots or flat versus aquiline noses or good hair versus bad hair or broad hips like a Mexican mango versus straight hips like an Anglo Saxon banana, were as foreign to Juan as the island of Cuba herself. In his eyes as an artist, there were truly no races and no general types, only people, individual people, who either made good or poor subjects for his scalpel and his brush. The notion of divisions among ethnic groups and races had a mythical ring in his ear, as when history teachers refer to the Chaldeans, or the Goths versus the Visigoths, for he had never felt part of a group.

Early on, he had encountered a poem by Walt Whitman that he thought spoke for him: "I hear it was charged against me that I sought to destroy institutions; / But really I am neither for nor against institutions; / (What indeed have I in common with them?—Or what with the destruction of them?)" His favorite answer whenever he was asked where he came from, ever since he was five and went to kindergarten in Coral Gables, was that he was an alien from an unknown galaxy. Once, in the sixth grade, he wrote in a paper that he was a Martian, but later changed it to Venusian because of the romantic sound of the word.

If Juan had been asked during those years between Yale and his twenty-ninth birthday—asked, for instance, by that detective and that district attorney he would never forget—what made sense to him in his life, what prompted him to go on in spite of his fits of melancholy and his fascination with the myriad modes of suicide, the way Arnaldo used to roll pebbles around in his mouth as an orphan child, he would have answered that it was, first, his dream of finding the woman behind the mirror—his north, his south, whichever—and then his art. Portrait painting, which he called art therapy, enabled him, while he worked and only while he worked, to eclipse the desolate thoughts that clung like clouds. It represented a great Zen exercise, where he'd mastered the art of peeling off his subjects' skin right down to the bone and then grafting them on to his canvas like the most skilled surgeon in the burn unit.

ArtNews had labeled his portraits a new form of Super Realism, a Super-Super Realism where even the most exact Nikon would fail. Only the light gave him away, the Equatorial light with intimations of Morpho and Ghost butterflies enveloping a subject who was either a Wall Street banker, a politician, or a Protestant clergyman you knew would never be at home among such climes. And the

71

light, this light which was nothing other than Esmeralda's far-flung breath on him and not his clinging to his roots, became his trademark. Critics wrote that his paintings had the quality of air orchids from the Amazon, and that their orris-root fragrance, their delicate, floating sepals cast a spell over western art. And when his paintings were auctioned at Christies or Sothebys, they fetched three and four times their original price because people said that Juan's magic had transcended his subjects three and four and many more times over.

Esmeralda's life, her undecipherable quotient, went along very separate lines from Juan's all those years. And yet it ran parallel where it counted, as she said, on the inside.

The days between her nineteenth and twenty-ninth birthdays were a white canvas painted white, with iridescent subaquatic colors in the pentimento underneath.

Although there seemed to be nothing in the way of progress along a straight line the way Juan's career went—and nothing the newspapers would want to write about where it concerned Esmeralda's life—still, inside her, in East Harlem, there ran a river as magical as Juan's paintings or Juan's vision before the mirror.

If Esmeralda had been asked the way Juan might have been asked—except she wasn't; the district attorney could never question her—what ran her life, she would have said it was first her love and pity for her father Arnaldo and her hope in her mother's resurrection. Next would be her friends, the butterflies, and the many dreams she had through them, including the dream of her other self, her dream of Juan (she did not know him by name, but they had had many conversations through the looking glass).

During the course of those years, Esmeralda had several jobs as a receptionist at beauty salons up and down Madison Avenue, and had several suitors like Mr. Sanders and Cristina exactly divided among the sexes. And she became even more active in her father's church, to the point of preaching the sermon and leading the altar calls on several occasions when her father took ill. Like Jesus, she grew in stature and in favor among men. She was liked at her jobs and adored by Arnaldo's parishioners. Most were recent Puerto Rican and Colombian immigrants and many had been delivered from the grip of drugs and alcohol by Arnaldo's laying-on of hands but as yet not from the claws of illiteracy or want.

And although Juan and Esmeralda lived in different worlds, they conducted the minutiae of their lives in such identical ways that someone watching them in a movie might think they were observing halves of the same screen. It was never in the obvious where their lives merged; it was in their secret way of seeing, in private tributaries that ran into their sea.

For example, on the outside Juan was a Don Juan, skilled at seduction and abandonment. But on the inside he saw himself a romantic who looked for love and never found it, a poet who would have been content with but one love if that one were the one for him. He saw himself a man ruled by dreams and all the water planets of the emotions.

And so to navigate between the two worlds, the fragile one of his imagination and the solid and opaque one of his life, Juan had constructed a carapace that kept everyone out. Everyone, that is, but the girl in the mirror. His dates with older women were appointments which he kept strictly for two hours at a time and not a minute longer. His meal times were ritualized. He was served only those things he liked in the order he liked, even if they seemed discordant in his grandmother's eyes. For example: mangos as appetizers; then fried plantains with bacon; then roast pork with papaya slices; then fried eggs with white rice; and, several Cokes for dessert. His friendships were carried out with a purpose: playing baseball or sailing a boat off Hialeah with some old roommate from Yale, or getting drunk on tequila *sangritas* or *Cuba Libres* with a wealthy patron who wanted his portrait hanging in Town Hall. And he steered clear of personal talk. His closets were built so precisely that the servants were forbidden to touch his clothes, and he hung his suits and his shirts alphabetically by designer, starting with Adolfo, his grandfather's favorite designer because he was, like him, another Cuban who had made it big.

The only times Juan felt at peace within his skin was when he painted or when he sensed Esmeralda's presence in the mirror. His favorite time was night, when he could lie on his Spanish-linen bed with the mahogany shutters opened wide and look up at the moon and the stars that cast their silvery light over Miami. He would see the visions Esmeralda was transmitting during her flights to the Equator with the Ghost and Morpho butterflies.

"I was constantly clearing my decks," he confessed to Esmeralda when they had begun comparing lives. "I guess I felt like I had to have a neat little compartment for each thing, including women and clothes. I firmly believed that people in general were the cause of my little black clouds, and I had to make sure they weren't really around in any meaningful way. Secretly, I was like some sort of virgin, always making room for you, Esmeralda. Mostly, I just wanted to lie in bed and think of you...or, I should say, think you."

That day Juan confessed how he'd organized his love life all those years, hung women in his mental closet, in the same way he had hung Adolfo and Armani under A and Bill Blass under B. He suddenly recalled a woman, a certain woman he'd known long ago, years before he finally met Esmeralda, and he was gripped by an old sadness, a mourning and repentance for those sins—which he did not call sins but errors—which can never be reversed. This woman, this certain woman he remembered was, in a sense, the embodiment and anatomy of all his love affairs. Her name was Barrett Brown, a Connecticut socialite of Confederate pedigree. She was platinum blonde and had eyes so watery blue and skin so wan that Juan, with his knack for condescension to the women he held in his sway, nicknamed her Albino Brown and showered her with broad-brimmed hats and blindman's glasses. And once, during a short trip to Hong Kong, brought her back a black parasol that hung all around her like a tent.

Barrett Brown was tall and swayed like an elegant reed in the breeze, always with one hand behind her waist propping up a hip and the other clutching her single strand of pearls which she wore everywhere, even to bed. She was softspoken, with a slight clench to the jaw and muffled mating coos under her ohs and ahs and other polite exclamations. She was also nearly forty when Juan was twenty-five and asked her to dance across the English-ivy and rambling-rose terrace where her husband, Juan's patron of the month, was hosting a party in honor of the congressman from Greenwich.

And because there was an age difference, and because she was married and by all appearances a seasoned, worldly woman who had long ago learned to keep her real heart in the vault while she exhibited the fake one, it might be presumed that Juan could do her no harm. But Juan knew the moment he captured her soft look and traced her thin, hungry lips with the tip of his finger what his remorse later told him. Here was no hard-bitten ice beauty with the manual for adultery engraved on her life line. Barrett was, in fact, a sincere intellectual, fragile like glass, sweet and finely tuned like a Mozart flute. No other kind of woman would ever capture his imagination.

She had known only her husband, whom she married at twenty after her return from Brazil and later Cambridge where she had studied anthropology and specialized in tribes of the Amazon.

She did not turn to Juan as a mere diversion, but as the man of her dreams, the one she had finally come to in the full flowering of her life. And Juan came to her as new territory to be conquered, as the land that perhaps at last would give him solace—although he doubted it, very much. Their summer romance went from high teas at the Carlyle to Bobby Shore whispering Mabel Mercer tunes at the Bemelmans Bar to a suite on the fourteenth floor overlooking Central Park that Barrett paid for. They kept the suite for three days straight without coming up for air, except for the few times they ordered room service, with Juan waiting in the bathroom so that Mrs. Brown would be perceived to be having dinner for two alone.

She did not look old to him, nor cold nor simply frigid, as his grandfather had once categorized all Anglo-Saxon women when he told him with fatherly advice that Nordic women could, by and large, iron your shirts, fry hamburgers and make love at the same time. In bed, Juan and Barrett shared remembered trips across Europe and the Alps. They sailed through Long Island Sound, hunted for mushrooms in Bavaria, went to dog races in Miami, and got drunk on Chinese beer at Jai-Alai games. Most of all, they shared their love of art. Barrett was a passionate lover of images. She needed only to close her eyes to view the greatest collections in the world, from the Hermitage to the Tate, as clearly as if each canvas, icon or marble torso had been etched with laser on her irises and blue pupils. Most of all, they shared her great addiction and her great eroticism for Juan, who needed the abject love and adoration of another to feel anything resembling appetite.

The louder she wailed in ecstasy under his watchful thrusts, the more Juan longed for love. The more she wept for joy and the higher her heart applauded his Oriental ability to sustain his manhood—although he did not call it ability, for he could not do otherwise and generally found surrender as difficult as some of the young virgins he had initiated—the more he wanted to drink her and smell her lily skin and sink in the folds of her flower. The more, that is, until the day he wanted no more.

It had happened so often that he could almost tell its symptoms, like the oncoming of the winter flu. First the chills, then the fever, the sneeze, the palpitating heart. Then the full-blown bug when everything ached and he had to take immediately to bed. And so, without so much as a word or a note, when the affair with Barrett Brown began its winter season in his heart, instead of subjecting himself to the usual gnashing of teeth and weeping through the dissecting loupe, the litigious reproaches, the dying swan scenes, the pinning and wriggling on the wall, Juan left suddenly for Miami and locked himself in the top floor of his Mizner. There, he consumed large bowls of fried plantains and drank Coca-Colas until the mental storm passed and his recent mistress would think of him no more.

Two weeks after his flight to Miami, Juan received a letter from a Yale friend announcing that Barrett Brown had taken her life. Some days later, he found an envelope from her husband under his door with no note, only fractured stanzas from a poem by Edna St. Vincent Millay which Barrett had copied in her finishing-school handwriting:

> ...Pity me not for beauties passed away
> ...Nor that a man's desire is hushed so soon...

...Pity me that the heart is slow to learn
What the swift mind beholds at every turn.

Esmeralda, on her part, was as precise and neat as Juan when it came to organizing her things, and she, too, had built a white egg shell around her mango so that those who came to her door could never carry her across the threshold. Like Juan, her days consisted of dreaming of the other, and, while comparing her life to Juan's, she concluded that her longing for the resurrection of her mother and her devotion to her father had been the equivalent of Juan's art, a duty that kept them anchored to this world until their destination was revealed.

Juan didn't have a God and Esmeralda had, in his eyes, too much God. Juan had never known what it was like to be hungry or feel his toes go numb in a rat-infested railroad flat. Yet, Esmeralda believed he had starved all his life for lack of the richness of the Spirit in his heart. Juan had embraced so many women he could not recall all of their names, and he had made such deep furrows in their wombs that the fruit of love could never grow again. Esmeralda had only known one man, and he was the one who had conceived them both. All this was also the counterpoint of their lives, the other side of their moon, the south and the north of them. Yet on that day when fate became as ripe as a blackened banana and Juan and Esmeralda finally met, these two points came together as one. The girl in the mirror became the man, and the man became the most fierce and passionate woman in the world.

SEVEN

At four on the Sunday morning of her twenty-ninth birthday, at the still point of the turning world, Esmeralda had a vision. Her visitors this time were not lizards or butterflies, but a large plumed owl and a donkey with eyes in the back of its head like the ones Perfecto, Arnaldo's first cousin, had once seen communing with him through the window.

And these visitors, whom she immediately named Marco and Mateo after the writers of the Gospels, spoke to her in white, silent voices that nonetheless sounded as loud as hurricanes and bore a birthday message. Later, when she was preaching from the pulpit, Esmeralda called it a revelation. The message was, simply, "Your day of discovery has come. Be not afraid, only obey."

And although Esmeralda could not fathom the full meaning of the missive, she understood that this day was like no other. When Arnaldo asked her to preach later that morning, Esmeralda had already prepared her sermon—which was never a sermon when she preached it, but rather a series of poetic incantations to refresh the thirsty souls of the parishioners.

Inside the Hot Mambo Social Club in front of Arnaldo's removable wooden cross and his purple and gold banner which read, *Jesus, Jesus, Jesus, El Nombre Más Dulce*, Esmeralda began to preach at eleven in the morning. There were eleven faithful that morning, including Arnaldo who sat in a chair behind the lectern. They were all holding their bilingual hymnals and singing *Come to the Church in the Vale*, waving their hands in the air, wiping their white handkerchiefs on Jesus' invisible face, waiting for the moment when the Spirit would move them to prophesy in tongues and be washed, once more, in the blood of the Lamb.

Esmeralda, who in her twenty-ninth year had ripened like a golden mango, was wearing a white pique dress to her ankles, pink satin ballerina slippers and a wreath of plastic lilies of the valley on the crown of her thick Arabian mane that cascaded all the way to her waist. She had developed a habit of standing still before the congregation, scanning their faces with her emerald eyes and simply waiting until the Spirit opened her mouth. Ever since she had begun preaching on a regular basis, she would stand there for five, ten minutes and hold the parishioners in mesmeric silence with her gaze until she felt the Spirit wave its railroad flag before her and motion her to preach.

Because of what the two heavenly creatures of the forest had prophesied, she waited inordinately long for a sign, wondering at first whether her revelation would come before or after the sermon. Finally, she was quickened and her words spread like a balm, like Mary Magdalene's alabaster jar, anointing the ears of the believers.

"Today I want us to close our eyes and see the Light before us, which you know is always looking at us even when we are not looking at it. I want us to think of Love. I said Love, my brothers and sisters. Not the love that makes people steal and cheat and kill and get drunk—because you know in your hearts the name of that love is not love, but hate— but the Love that glues together the petals of a flower. The Love that brings together your top lip with your bottom lip when you speak. The Love that gives us a good push out of bed when we wake up in the morning and keeps us moving on the subway, even when your *jefe* at the *factoría* spat next to you and took the Lord's name in vain and cheated you out of overtime that day. I'm talking about the kind of Love that Jesus felt for the man with the withered hand and for the woman with the issue of blood and for the lepers and for the crazy man with demons jumping up and down inside of him.

"I'm talking about the kind of Love Jesus felt for his disciples and the kind of Love he feels for every one of us here. And for your *mamasitas* and for your *papasitos* back in Cali or Mayagüez, whether they're in this world or in the next. And for every creature on this planet, including His beautiful butterflies and His mango and banana and coconut trees, and even for the little tiny ants and insects that crawl all around us and we don't even see.

"And when you think about this Love, this big-time Love I'm talking about, then begin to feel it. I mean, begin to let this Love take over your lives now. And then, begin to let this Love be the power in your lives. Begin to let this Love be your shield and buckler, your guardian angel, your big *machete*, your tall palm tree, your panama hat, your great big *mantilla* to keep you from all harm. Any kind of harm..."

Suddenly, while the faithful were clapping their hands in the air and shouting Amen and Praise the Lord; while they were tilting their heads in the direction Esmeralda moved, from left to right and up and down as she pointed with her particular index-finger gesture that always reminded Arnaldo of the way Fidel addressed a crowd, Esmeralda stopped cold in her tracks.

A vision had begun to overtake her. But rather than one in human or animal form, the picture before her eyes was a long black funnel, like a typhoon gathering strength and coming straight at her from the middle of the ocean. Suddenly, she perceived she was preparing for an advent that, without a doubt, meant completion. At first Esmeralda thought it was her mother Patricia's resurrection, and enormous fear and exhilaration began to rattle her the way fear used to squeeze her throat years before, running on her tracks like the Lexington Avenue IRT. All at once she knew it could not be Patricia, because that would have to be Arnaldo's miracle and not hers. Also, this particular revelation was happening to her and not him. He was sitting still behind her in a worldly reality, unaware of the typhoon traveling like a meteor and preparing to crash on the Hot Mambo Social Club to ignite a fire in her brain.

"I perceive the Spirit moving among us today in a very special way. Maybe because today is my birthday and the Lord has prepared a gift for us," she said calmly, letting herself speak only the words the Spirit whispered. She felt her friends the Morpho and Ghost butterflies gathering around her like angels. "As I look around this room, our church, this place where God brings us together to worship and respect His universe, I count and I see that there are eleven among us. And I ask myself, where is the twelfth? Where is the twelfth disciple who is needed today to complete this ring of Love, to pour down the great blessings God has in store for us, pressed down, shaken together and running over, like showers from the great heavenly Light..."

As Esmeralda spoke, her voice grew stronger. Soon the congregation had risen spontaneously and lifted the palms of their hands to the chipped plaster ceiling. They began praising God and speaking in tongues. Suddenly, Esmeralda heard the front door unlatch and she counted the slow footsteps of a man who, when he stood before her in the aisle, looked up at the makeshift altar and fixed his large green eyes on hers. She immediately understood that he was Juan Saavedra, her twin soul, her other.

Early that morning, Juan awoke in a room at the Carlyle Hotel in Manhattan. He could not remember how he'd gotten there or what he was doing in New York, since his grandfather was throwing a large birthday party for him at their country club in Miami that evening. At first, he thought he might have had too much to drink the night before and had boarded a plane for New York in a blackout. But he touched his head and it did not hurt. And his stomach, rather than feeling nauseous as it often felt in the morning even when he'd had nothing to drink, felt like nothing at all. That is, Juan sensed he didn't have a stomach, or a head or a liver or a heart at all. He was light as a feather on the bed. He was an insubstantial creature who nonetheless was there, impelled by a strange energy that enabled him to move from place to place in the room by just thinking himself there without exercising a single muscle.

When he stood before the bathroom mirror, holding a disposable Gillette in his hand, Juan saw that his cheeks and his prominent jaw were shining and razor clean, and that every thick black strand of hair on his head was in place, wetted down and combed to the left. As he put the razor down on the sink, confused and yet not really alarmed, he accidentally cut his left hand and, having hit a vein that ran all the way to his wrist watch, he began bleeding profusely. The blood splashed his entire arm and the marble sink like a bottle of cologne that had suddenly slipped from his hand. Rather than feeling faint at the sight of the blood, Juan was suddenly bathed in a thick, blinding light that, he later explained, separated him from all the objects of existence, including his body, which he viewed as an object, as a material apart from him.

Following this momentary immersion in light and this total separation from the world, he felt that if he directed his thoughts to the gash, the bleeding would stop. He did, and the bleeding stopped instantaneously. He did not experience pain nor the burning sensation of the blade.

Afterwards, Juan found himself fully dressed in a pale gray Armani suit, a white shirt, and a red and silver tie which he had apparently packed in his suitcase but did not remember owning. He sat down at the foot of the bed and waited for a sign. He was not afraid, but he experienced the nervous anticipation of a father before the birth of his daughter, or of a mother who has been told her son is home from war. But since he had never been in the habit of praying and felt no particular connection to a spiritual world—other than Esmeralda's apparitions in the full-length mirror—he stared blankly into the television screen like a child waiting to be picked up by his parents at a railroad station, careful of strangers, reading the timetables on the electronic board over and over.

The missive came shortly before eleven in the morning, when Esmeralda and Arnaldo were already setting up the chairs for the congregants and hanging the purple banner and the wooden cross on the wall. Instead of appearing in the form of a large plumed owl or a donkey, the way it had come to Esmeralda, Juan's message came on a tiny slip of paper he found in his shirt pocket. In his own handwriting was scribbled: 221 East 111th Street, New York City.

The moment he saw it, he knew that was where he had to go. And he felt in his heart that if he went, he would find out why he had come and how he had come and perhaps even where he was going.

When Juan opened the door of the Hot Mambo Social Club and found his other, Esmeralda, the girl in the mirror, he knew why he had come and he understood that finding her at last was not so much a beginning as a continuation of a story begun long ago.

Juan was called to the altar not only by Esmeralda and Arnaldo—who did not recognize him, but saw him as a stranger who had wandered in—but by the happy congregation who felt immediately this man had been sent from above. And he went willingly to kneel before Esmeralda and Arnaldo, to feel their laying-on of hands on his moist head and to proclaim, although he didn't have the slightest understanding of their meaning, that on that day, on his twenty-ninth birthday, he was willing to give his life to Jesus and be born again. He was not moved by their singing or by their clapping and shouting out Biblical names. Nor was he, as his friends and grandmother and grandfather would have been, alarmed, revolted or amused. He had been brought here for an appointment with fate and was willing to suffer the rituals, if by suffering them, it meant that he could say, as he remembered the first line in *Doctor Zhivago*, "And on they went."

EIGHT

And on they went, Juan and Esmeralda, not really knowing where life was leading them, to a future that seemed to be their antecedent.

Of the mechanical world on the outside, of the way they conducted themselves at their first meeting, it could be said to be the shadow play of new lovers everywhere. Their hearts knew at a glance not really what they were—a twin brother and sister born in Cuba and separated at birth—but who they were. And they knew that regardless of their different stations and beliefs or the way they had oriented their faces towards heaven or hell, north or south, they wanted nothing more than to be facing each other now.

Juan had always been the most reluctant of lovers; he automatically checked the exits before entering. And when he entered, it was always because he was beckoned and begged, never out of spontaneous volition. He heard himself say words that he would have privately laughed at if, in his life before Esmeralda, he had heard a man say them in a movie or in a line to a movie theater, which was just where he voiced what his heart felt for the first time.

"I want to squeeze the universe into a ball," he told her, using T.S. Eliot, whom Esmeralda had never read or heard about, "and place it all at your feet, Esmeralda. More than frankincense and myrrh, more than all of King Solomon's treasures, I wish to bring everything that's beautiful to you. You who are the most beautiful."

And this medieval profession of love, this courtly Spanish gesture that came out of he knew not where, but which no doubt had been part of his psyche and part of the way his Cuban roots, even those denied, spread wide across the Atlantic and back to the Iberian Peninsula of his ancestors, met an equal response from Esmeralda.

"And I to you, Juan. I want to give all I have, not only with my heart, but with my friends, the butterflies, who I believe have been our telephone line."

The first day, after church, Juan helped put away the chairs and bring down the wooden cross. He then mingled with the parishioners, who were surprised that a rich Cuban, an *exilado* in a fancy suit, would be interested in Jesus when he probably had the Pope's ear. They nevertheless regarded him as an omen, a lucky sign that money would soon come their way. In the eyes of many, including Arnaldo, money begat money, and if a rich man walked in the door, money followed him like a battalion of soldiers, dropping gold coins like bread crumbs for pigeons in his path.

Ricardo Maldonado, a Puerto Rican who was a carpenter by trade, was the first to ask Juan to tell him his favorite numbers. And before the group dispersed an hour later, after Cuban coffee and *cuchifritos* which Esmeralda served the believers on Sunday mornings, everyone had privately asked Juan to whisper a few numbers in their ears.

They insisted that he blurt them out as they occurred to him, without really thinking, because that was the way the Spirit communicated with people most accurately, by by-passing their reason and memory, which tended to taint the message with temporal lies such as birthdays, their addresses, or when their children were baptized.

After the service, the four men and five women present bought New York State Lotto tickets for that Wednesday's drawing with the numbers Juan had given them. Ricardo Maldonado placed a bet for *la bolita* in Arnaldo's name, even though he had been warned by Arnaldo to forsake his bookie because it meant gambling, which was one of the many ills he had been healed of when Jesus saved him.

Arnaldo and Juan exchanged a few words, but Arnaldo seemed preoccupied that first day with a sharp pain in his head which had prevented him from preaching that morning and other Sundays during the past six months. There seemed to be no click, no connection or recognition between Arnaldo and his son, who nonetheless looked almost identical to his own daughter and his beloved Patricia. It seemed as though whenever Arnaldo looked into Juan's face, a mist rose before it and he could not really break down his features or sense his presence in the way he was used to discerning people's thoughts since age sixteen when the Methodist missionary had called him to the altar.

On his part, Juan felt no particular affinity to Arnaldo and regarded him rather as the help that hung around his house in Key Biscayne begging for work—like Pablo the gardener, or Miguel, the Marielito who cleaned and prepped his sailboat. It was hard for Juan to imagine how a man as simple and undernourished-looking as Arnaldo could be the father of a woman who shined with so much grace and beauty. In fact, he thought that if his grandmother María met Arnaldo, she would send him a box of Vitamin B-12, the way she had done to so many Marielitos whom she believed to be suffering from a vitamin B deficiency—a belief which ran rampant among the Cuban exile community in Miami.

When the crowd dispersed, Arnaldo was ready to take his daughter home and, as was his custom on Sundays, lie on her sofa bed and watch the soccer game on Channel 41 while she prepared *arroz con pollo* or, his favorite, squid with rice and fried plantains. Juan asked if he might have a talk with Esmeralda about being born again. And Arnaldo, who on this day was eager to nurse his headache (which felt more like a sword in his head than an ache) with *hierba buena* and other herbs from the *botánica* across the street, released his daughter to go alone with Juan and tell him of her personal encounter with the Lord.

Esmeralda knew this first meeting with Juan was not about the Lord, but about them, for she had recognized him as soon as he had unlatched the door. What her body was beginning to undergo in his presence was so different from anything she'd ever felt before, that she became fascinated by the changes happening inside her at the precise moment she stood beside him in the Hot Mambo Social Club.

Esmeralda felt the veins in her neck swell and her blood heat like water in a test tube under flame. She felt her knees soften and go limp, like coconuts ready to drop. She felt a large palpitating heart in her flower and a hot river of love running out from her the minute Juan put his arm across her shoulders and escorted her into the street.

Juan was overtaken by immediate and insurmountable desire for Esmeralda before he could utter a word or carry on a civil conversation. The minute they were alone on One Hundred and Eleventh Street, walking towards he knew not where, he was seized by a longing so great to enter her, to kiss her flesh, and to possess her for all time. He led her into an abandoned building which a band of crack free-basers used as cover. On the floor of a back room with plaster walls caved-in to the wire and the stench of urine and human defecation everywhere, he placed her on his jacket, fell on her, and came inside her without a sound or a word spoken. His ardor combined the fierceness of a lover who has found his mate with the gentleness of butterflies on silent flights to their hidden Equator.

Juan and Esmeralda stayed there, joined together on that abandoned floor, inventing their lovemaking, a hard lovemaking, fierce and importunate, that suited their yearning and their halves and no one else's. They clung to each other's lips, their identical pomegranate lips, and breathed each other's breath, their identical syncopated breath, until night fell around them and they emerged as one.

That night after the dinner and the movie— *Black Orpheus*, one of Juan's favorites, which was playing at the Biograph—they began to open the album of their lives and compare notes like remembered photographs. Juan asked Esmeralda to spend the night at the Carlyle and then fly back with him to Miami the next day where, like the passionate shepherd to his love, she could come and live with him and be his love and they would all the pleasures prove. But Esmeralda, who felt the seams of her lining were now forever intertwined with Juan's and who had just awakened to desire for the first time, heeded the commandment to honor her father and go home.

Juan walked her to her doorstep at One Hundred and Seventeenth Street. He knew the things of the outward world did not conform to their separate reality but must be accepted until he and his lover found the key that would unlock the door they could forever close behind them, leaving the world to fall off its own edge.

The things Juan and Esmeralda had talked about that day in between the kisses and the ardent clinging and the many times he came inside her with his ravenous member, which was as large and as ready as his father Arnaldo's when his heart had swallowed Patricia whole, were the things they took with them that night to think about and understand while they lay on separate beds, forty-four blocks apart, under the same starless sky. They had compared notes as far back as their memories would take them. And the things that struck them were not only the discovery of each other in the mir-

ror, or the day and hour they both realized there
was another, or that that part of them lived north
or south. They recalled the little things, as Esmeralda called them, that seemed to form the fila-
ments and fabric of their future meetings, the signs
that foretold them but which back then neither one
could possibly suppose.

"Did you know that I fell in the East River
when I was ten and nearly drowned, and that a
woman, who was six feet tall with long blond hair
and purple eyes, jumped in and saved me?" Esmeralda told Juan.

Amazed, Juan had answered, "And did you
know that when I was ten I fell off a boat in Key
West and that a woman, who was six feet tall with
blond hair and purple eyes and who was whizzing
by on a kayak, jumped in and saved my life!"

Then they went on to compare the times when
they both had measles—on the same day and time—
and the night a ruby-throated hummingbird came
into their bedrooms, pecked their lips and flew away
through a closed window. And the times they had
dreamt the same dreams—riding a pink horse
through a mangled grove; flying over Cuba in a bal-
loon; eating mangos and coconuts in the Bosque de la
Habana, a place neither one had ever seen; chopping
cane and visiting Fidel at Varadero Beach, another
place they had never seen; and then, the most pecu-

liar dream of all, the one that kept recurring year by year: Patricia.

For Juan, she had appeared in his dreams not as Patricia but as a silver angel clad in white with large green eyes like his. She held him to her breast and helped him weep the tears he could not weep, especially during the years he was away in military school where boys were forbidden to cry.

For Esmeralda, she was her own mother, who came in the night and whispered that she loved her, and who she prayed someday would come back altogether and settle down with her and her father in East Harlem. But for both, Patricia was the presence that gave them comfort in the dark.

There were also many other occurrences which would be classified by unbelievers as coincidences, such as the time they won school prizes or met a black dog named Jellybean or went to the circus and were abducted by a clown who later released each one unharmed with a note that read "Take Better Care Of Your Children."

And the memory of their parallel lives and those things others might call coincidences, including the ones they had yet to uncover, were the blocks that built the path from which they could never return. But in all their explorations and in spite of knowing that they had both been born in Oriente province and brought to America at an almost identical age, and seeing how they looked alike even down to the soft black hair on the backs of their necks and how even a stranger would guess that they were probably twins, Esmeralda and Juan never considered that possibility.

They were riveted on each other as the lovers they were destined to be and not as the brother and sister that had been born to Arnaldo and Patricia long ago when Arnaldo was the town shaman and his skin was golden like a mango and Patricia was the richest and most beautiful young woman in the province.

That first night when Esmeralda came home, Arnaldo was already asleep in his cot. His headache had kept him from wondering about her, for this was the first time she had stayed away so many hours. So the nervousness she felt at the thought of having to explain and then having to lie for the first time was removed—removed, that is, until the middle of the night. For that night, Arnaldo, who no longer made it his practice to slip into her bed every night, came to visit her as he had done all the years before, presenting himself naked at her side, holding her to him with stories of his past. But this time Esmeralda had discovered what love was and had exchanged her heart with Juan's. She could no longer do what she had done for so many years. She could no longer be the vessel for her father's sorrow or the repository of his sad, misguided longing.

When Arnaldo appeared, Esmeralda, who had been dreaming of Juan, bolted suddenly from her bed and without thinking stood up, looked straight at her father, and said, "I cannot do this anymore, Papá. I know you mean well, but there are other things in my life I must think about, too..."

"Such as what? What can you think about that does not include your devotion to your father Arnaldo?" he asked, feeling like Adam, suddenly embarrassed at his nakedness before his daughter. For in all those years she had never looked at him and they had only touched under the covers.

Esmeralda, realizing his embarrassment and feeling shame herself as well as that old invincible pity for her father, responded, "Nothing...nothing that can't include you, Papá.... It's just that I don't feel very well and I'd rather be left alone tonight."

"Very well, my daughter," answered Arnaldo, covering his loins with the T-shirt he had dropped on the floor and returning to his bed.

An hour later, while both father and daughter lay awake in their apartment on One Hundred and Seventeenth Street, each wondered what the other thought and each dreamed private dreams. The image of Juan could never leave Esmeralda for an instant, and Patricia's face haunted Arnaldo every night. Arnaldo finally spoke up. His disembodied voice seemed to hang over her like a levitated chair, but it would soon descend on her with the full impact of its material weight.

"Was it that young man who came to church today? Is that what's made you turn your father away?"

"No." Esmeralda reasoned that she must lie and that she must be sparse in her lying, for she was sure Arnaldo could always read her thoughts.

"You must remember, my little Esmeralda, that the Devil comes in many guises, and that he would tempt us in the flesh. Above all in the flesh. That young man, for instance, a rich young man who walks into our neighborhood and says he wants Jesus...but does he really want Jesus? What is it that he wants? Has he come to tempt my daughter? Is he who he says he is, or is he Satan in a shiny suit?"

"He's a Cuban from Miami who was led by the Spirit to come to our church and accept Jesus. That's all I know about him. He took your mimeographed sheet on the Duties of the Believer and bought a Bible." Esmeralda could feel her voice quiver. In all her twenty-nine years she had honored her father. She had never lied to him. She had never denied him anything.

"And what are the Duties of the Believer, Esmeralda? Can you recount them for your father?" Arnaldo had an edge to his voice Esmeralda had never heard before. His inflection had always been smooth and round when he spoke to her, as light as the soft pebbles she learned to skip in Central Park. And now there was a hidden dagger in his cloak.

Esmeralda closed her eyes and summoned her friends, the butterflies. When one appeared and fluttered on her forehead, she answered Arnaldo: "Thou shalt honor your father and your mother until the day you die and take care of them and give thanks every day that you are not an orphan. And if you are an orphan, give thanks that the Lord Jesus died for you and loves you and that there is one father, God.

"Thou shalt not lie, steal, curse, commit adultery, think bad thoughts about other people unless they deserve rebuke like the money changers in the temple and you are told so by the Lord Jesus Christ.

"Thou shalt not have anything to do with unbelievers.

"Thou shalt not be yoked with lazy people or eat without saying grace, or eat too much, or drink too much or gamble or do drugs which is the Devil's work.

"And thou shalt do honest work and pay for your rent and not freeload on your relatives or friends or lean on your wife or your in-laws to support you.

"And thou shalt bring up your child in the Lord Jesus, instructing him in the way that he should go, and not spare the rod if it's necessary, but always being careful not to hurt him too much.

"And thou shalt be kind to animals and little things that don't know any better.

"And thou shalt be clean in all things and not do the stupid things that sinners do and get sick in the inward parts."

"Good," said Arnaldo. "Remember those things, Esmeralda. Hold them fast to your heart so you can be ready before the great Tribulation and the Lord Jesus can then feel you're worthy of being lifted in the air during the Rapture."

" Yes, Papá."

NINE

The words in Cuba and in most of Latin America were *casa grande* and *casa chica*. *Casa grande* was the main house, where the husband lived with his wife and children, and *casa chica* was the small house, where he kept his mistress and supported their love children. The *casa chica* always knew about the *casa grande*, but the *casa grande* did not always know of the *casa chica*. If a man was manly or had achieved a certain station in life, it would be reasonable for the wife to assume he kept a *casa chica* somewhere in another part of town.

Juan decided to take up residence in Manhattan, in Carnegie Hill on Ninety-First and Madison, on the top floor of a brownstone with a glass skylight that provided the fire he needed for his portraits, although not quite the light he found in Miami, which he preferred for what he called a harlot's shameless and unmerciful sky. He never thought that it was, in fact, a *casa chica* which he was setting up for himself and Esmeralda. But in the end he told himself that *that* was what it had turned out to be, a kind of inverted *casa chica* where Juan starred as the mistress and Arnaldo played the cuckold husband.

After that night when she first lied to Arnaldo, Esmeralda could not find it in her heart to break away. Not because she did not love Juan, but because she discovered, after attempting to cut the life chord that tied her to her father, that her own lining and sinews and heart muscle were also sewn tightly to Arnaldo's. So tightly that to pull away might be to sever something as vital as the superior vena cava or the golden thread that wove her to life itself. No matter how she tried to picture it, she could not see herself leaving behind Arnaldo, a sad and lonely man whose life revolved around her and the memory of her mother. And she could not see herself telling him the truth, for that implied betrayal. And she could not see herself without Arnaldo, for as difficult as it might have been for Juan to comprehend, Arnaldo had been her bedrock all those years, the solid land on this vast gulf of a native and yet foreign country that, while possessing her, was still not possessed by her.

And Juan, understanding (but not knowing of Esmeralda's nights with Arnaldo, for she had never told him), set up his *casa chica*, thinking of himself as the mistress who would someday reap the reward of her patience when her lover finally announced his divorce or killed his wife or left her the coward's way, without bidding farewell.

Beginning that month of May when Juan and Esmeralda met, Esmeralda's days were split into two halves of a coconut, one for her nights and one for her days, until the afternoon when the twisted hand of Fate that had started its way long ago back in Oriente province on the eve of Fidel's rising, knocked on her door with a black velvet glove.

Her day-life began when she left the railroad apartment on One Hundred and Seventeenth Street in the morning, telling Arnaldo she was off to work at the beauty salon on Madison Avenue. Instead she went straight down to her love nest in Carnegie Hill, to the cleanest and most orderly square block in town, with ivy and geranium window boxes adorning the freshly hosed streets and Standard Poodles walking with servants on retractable leads. It was a neighborhood she had actually never visited until now. Here, there were no *bodegas* and no shirtless men holding up beer cans in paper bags and squatting up against the walls of buildings, and no boys in neon caps and pumped-up sneakers blasting their Spanglish rap and salsa music, craving for sex, money and drugs.

Juan convinced Esmeralda to quit her job and let him pay her salary, an offer Esmeralda readily accepted, for she saw this as the only way to satisfy both halves of the coconut. She reasoned that although Juan was not a job—for how could loving him and giving herself to him be a job—he was certainly a duty, a duty that her heart had been entrusted to fulfill long ago, even, perhaps, long before they emerged as human beings on this planet.

During those early days, which they swore to remember always, frame by frame, it was Esmeralda and Juan, Juan and Esmeralda, with the rest of the world as their oyster and backdrop. They spent hours in his brass bed on fresh white Pratesi sheets, surrounded by white lilies and yellow orchids and red birds of paradise Juan had ordered from Renny by the dozens. Often they lunched at Equense or Sarabeth's in the neighborhood, and then Juan showed her the Metropolitan Museum. They carefully studied each room and collection on separate days so that each would be remembered then recollected and savored in tranquility when they lay in one another's arms and Juan made love to her imagining himself pressing on her against Caravaggio's Lute Player or rolling on Monet's orange water lilies across the floor of the Walter Annenberg Collection.

This sudden change of telescope for Esmeralda, this viewing life from the distant star of one who has never lacked for riches or beauty or the fragrance of spring or Equatorial bulbs or brocade fabrics that swell under index and thumb, did not awaken in her a lust for worldly possessions or a pity for her and her father's lot. Nor did it engender a sense that, compared to Juan's, her life, which had seemed so full until now, was an empty beggar's tin cup.

The things which Esmeralda dreamt about and cherished in their love were not things but moments which could not be described by life in the three-dimensional world of brass frames and paintings and flowers or even clean white Italian bedding. They were the moments which emerged from their passionate and hungry lovemaking, from the explosion and fusion of their hearts. They were not the moments of desire and then overwhelming fulfillment. For Esmeralda, their sacred moments were the times of their oneness and ascension. At those still points of the turning world Juan and Esmeralda cracked their carapace bodies wide open and split their hearts in two, each one reflecting the other, and communed with her friends, the butterflies, and fed the lizards kisses from their lips and floated up, unfettered by their relative existence into a magic, incorporeal world which was, to her way of seeing things, the only verifiable reality. Juan had described those moments as the times when her reality erased his with a white paint-roller, and he gave himself to her like an empty canvas. Esmeralda had explained them as the times when the Spirit honored them the way it says in the Ninety-First Psalm that the Lord will honor the

psalmist because he has set his love upon Him, because he has known His name, because both Juan
and Esmeralda had dwelled in the secret place of
the most High. To her, it was the Lord's way of giving back, of inviting them onto His throne for short
flashes of time.

Juan explained it as the magic spell she had
cast on him from the beginning and for which she
and her witches, the butterflies, were exclusively
responsible. Although he refrained from discussing
theology or anything that took them from emotion
into logic—which he despised because it had never
brought him any solace—he felt he had no god. And
if he ever had one, he would prefer it be Esmeralda,
whom he at least trusted and loved with all his
human heart.

"Look deeply at this little scrap of air," Esmeralda would often start just before they began their
journey with her blue Ghost and Morpho butterflies, making Juan concentrate by looking up at the
sky through the glass in his skylight, "and tell me
what you see."

At first Juan might see light centipedes crawling skyward, or single cell amoeba in flashes of
green and yellow light, or little sun dots in a row,
such as the ones he used to trap under his eyelids
in Miami as a child when he closed his eyes tight
after staring at the sun. Esmeralda called this the
stage of opening your heart to the little world that

turns into the big world. She led him with her voice, whispering in his ear, breathing rapidly against his neck, rubbing her lips across the back of his head, licking him with her lizard tongue and squeezing her thumbs against his buttocks until he began to feel her invincible sensuality and strength envelop him like the red satin cape of the matador.

And soon, Juan began seeing Esmeralda's butterflies swarm through the sealed glass ceiling in random and colorful formations, organizing themselves in phalanxes around them, taking first an arm, then a leg, then the whole length of his spine and suspending him horizontally in midair, in his apartment on Carnegie Hill, on the Isle of Manhattan. Once Juan was airborne, Esmeralda, too, would be lifted by her friends, the butterflies with their powerful, invisible beams of light. In seconds, Esmeralda would become nothing but green, and Juan would feel as transparent as the thin air in Machu Picchu. They would take up their journey, first over Manhattan where people and ants were exactly the same—both infinitely small and incredibly large and defined right down to their floating vertebrae and the microscopic cilia in their noses— and then down to Equatorial rivers where their flights mimed the course of giant fish in the muddy Amazon and where blue speckled parrots fanned their feathers in their path. They flew together as one, and whatever river or jasmine breeze or mango fruit would flow through the channel of their veins was the same for both. And both felt as charged and as mighty as tropical electric storms.

Juan knew during those times that his own body lay asleep somewhere at the foot of the bed on Madison and Ninety-First and that Esmeralda, if someone were suddenly to open the door, would be found not far from him, asleep, perhaps clutching his sex or tugging at his toes. But during those moments he felt that this was his real life, incorporeal, floating above the rivers and the forests, exercising his spirit and his oneness with this woman who was none other than his twin self. He told Esmeralda he felt invulnerable during their flights, capable of knowing and healing all, worthy of sitting at the dinner table with Esmeralda's part-Hebrew, part-African god.

Arnaldo knew Esmeralda could heal, and he had seen her rescue a choke victim at church with a simple glance. But it surprised him to discover that he, too, possessed her powers, although he felt he possessed them to a lesser degree. Once, after their souls had returned and fit themselves back in their human frames, while he was walking Esmeralda home, he saw a child on a bicycle collide and then slide under the wheels of a U-Haul truck. Without considering what he should do, Juan threw himself on the tiny fractured body enveloped in blood, pulled him out, laid his hands on him and seared his wounds, rendering him completely whole long before the ambulance and the doctors came.

"That was the Lord's power operating in you, Juan," Esmeralda told him as they walked away leaving the child stunned and the passers-by with hanging jaws. "And my father has told me that whenever we're given the gift of healing, we should give thanks and acknowledge that we're not doing it ourselves. That it's the work of the Lord Jesus."

But Juan did not ponder her words. At that moment, he felt unaware of what he'd done, as if a hand had guided him and he had been a witness, but never the healer himself.

One night, after Esmeralda had gone and was lying on the bed next to her father, Juan began to reconstruct their life and wonder how his grandfather Mario and his grandmother María would explain his incorporeal migrations with Esmeralda and his out-of-body flights after lovemaking which, day by day, became more real to him, more real than his life back in Miami where he spent the days sinking in despair, hiding under the bed, and consuming Coca-Colas and fried plantains. This new life was more real than his long rosary chain of married women and all his other country-club escapades. It was even more real than his paintings, which he now saw as mere portraits of vain people in mad quests for human immortality.

"These things which you describe to me," he could hear Don Mario Ona tell him, "are no more than trance states induced by heightened stages of sexual pleasure and indulgence. A mental masturbation, if you will. And they are part of your south, the tragic element, the slightly crazy touch that makes it possible for you to paint so well."

Juan laughed out loud, feeling sure Don Mario would say exactly that. Arnaldo wished he could tell Don Mario of the way his life had changed since Esmeralda, but realizing he had to wait until the time came for her to free herself, he would wait for the right moment to bring her to Miami to become his wedded wife.

Part of him doubted what he lived with Esmeralda—particularly at night, after she had flown away. Part of him still wanted to believe in reason, the reason his grandfather had instilled in him: the Doubting-Thomas cynicism that Don Mario told Juan had made him rich and kept him sane in spite of Fidel Castro's revolution. But then the sun came in through the glass ceiling. And with the sun came Esmeralda. And with her, a magic and a power that could not be denied.

"Close your eyes and what do you see," Esmeralda asked him early one morning while pouncing on him to wake him.

"A red parrot," Juan answered, pulling her against his chest.

"And what else… C'mon, c'mon, answer quickly without thinking, because thinking spoils the game!"

"A pair of tennis shoes walking on water by themselves…and my mother María chasing after them…"

"And, quickly, what else!"

"A girl with green eyes walking in the night on a sugar plantation, in Cuba, by herself…"

They had entered his dream, the one she found him quivering his eyelids over. Esmeralda knew it. He followed her.

"What is she wearing and what is she doing? Quickly, just say it without thinking! Let your dreams tell you!"

"She's wearing a white dress. She's walking in cloth slippers. She's entering a tiny thatched hut in the moonlight… She's kissing a man, a man who looks somewhat like your father… A man who *is* your father!"

Suddenly, they stopped. Esmeralda asked Jesus how it was possible for Juan to dream about her mother Patricia. Juan wondered how he could possibly be dreaming her dreams. And still, looking like mirrored reflections of each other, Juan and Esmeralda could not see beyond the Shekinah of their lover's sleep. It would take more than Esmeralda's morning game to awaken them.

TEN

"Back in Oriente, if a man needed a hand from an *amigo*, a real *amigo*, all he had to do was show up at his doorstep and he'd be asked in for a plate of rice and beans," Arnaldo said to a man named Hector who was leaning against the bar at the Loma Linda Coctel Bar on Lenox Avenue. Hector was sipping straight, dark Bacardi shots, sticking his index finger in the glass, sucking it and then rubbing it under the gum beneath his upper lip. "But in this cold, cold country," Arnaldo continued, "you have to go to a bar and talk to strangers if you need to get anything off your chest."

Arnaldo had been there three hours, ever since he finished his rounds of the buildings on his block at two in the afternoon. The man named Hector, who used to harvest cane in the Dominican Republic and now drove a gypsy cab in Washington Heights, was already the third amigo Arnaldo had informed of his views of life in the United States.

"Well, I'm no stranger," the man named Hector replied, ignoring the short glass and drinking his Budweiser straight from the can, "because in this country we're all brothers and we have to stick together because, after all, they call us *hispanos*, don't they? To them we're all the same. Okay? We're all the children of the same Spick parents who fucked like rabbits, don't you know?"

Arnaldo knew the man named Hector was slurring and he understood that no matter what he told him, he would not remember Arnaldo's words once he got in his gypsy cab later that night. The thought that he could speak his mind, that he could let that trapped, angry canary fly out of his heart without fear of being punished for his thoughts against a country which, after all, had taken him in and labeled him a political refugee when the Ona dogs were raging after him, gave him much comfort. It kept him coming back to the Loma Linda Coctel Bar, where no one knew him as a minister and a man of God, but only as a janitor and part-time sanitation man. The Loma Linda was his destination whenever his soul felt troubled, so troubled that he wished he could board a plane back to Santiago and knock on his cousin Perfecto's open door and be invited in for a heaping plate of black or pinto beans.

There had been a few times throughout the years while Esmeralda was growing up that Arnaldo had felt that angry trapped canary in his heart. Those had been the times when he was afraid of losing his job and starving or having to show up at the Welfare office like a mangy dog with his little daughter in his arms. The times when his King James English failed him with the Irish or Italian bosses. The times he felt like a sand pebble floating in a tar and cement city where taking a siesta cost you money and where his loneliness for his Patricia was so deep and his dismay at the thought of Esmeralda all by herself in school, surrounded by unchaste and lustful men, was so great that he felt the Lord Jesus had taken a vacation back to Cuba, leaving him stranded, bleeding from the ribs, holding up his cross.

But this time, what brought Arnaldo to the Loma Linda Coctel Bar was less concrete yet more troublesome than before. He had not been here in months, and the moment he looked in the mirror and saw his gaunt face, his prematurely wrinkled cheeks and yellow brow, his hazel eyes the color of dusty plums, he knew somewhere inside him there was a message, a sealed envelope with a terrible truth he had not yet been able to rip open. What that message was about, he could only suspect. And suspecting was as frightening as finally splitting that coconut truth wide open. So, instead he came to the watering hole like a sad mule, the "sad mule with budding testicles" as his dead grandmother had called him just before she died of a strangulated hernia. He came here to hear the sound of his own voice and talk with other poor, transplanted men, *yucas* or sweet potatoes that like him could not yield proper fruit in this frigid, rocky soil called Nueva York. Like him, they needed to flex their self-respect, the kind of self-respect that told them that no matter how Pigmy-short or shit-dark or ignorant they seemed to the Anglos whose streets they swept and whose latrines they cleaned, in each other's eyes they still were *hombres, machos* after all.

"If you want to know why this country is going to hell in a hand basket with all the Yanquis in it, and with us *hispanos*, too," said the man named Hector, "you can just blame it on the fact that all politicians around the world, from Mexico City to Bayamon, are thieves, including Clinton. And the air and the soil, the type of air and soil you get in this country turns women into whores and shrivels up your balls. And the water here, even the water in the Hudson River that comes out of your faucet, has cancer running in it."

"You think Clinton is a thief, too?" asked Arnaldo, who held a certain respect for the American president because he had read in *El Diario* that in spite of his transgressions, he was a man of God.

"No doubt about it," answered the man named Hector, gulping his Budweiser and gesturing for another to the bartender on the other side. "Didn't you just read where he's giving all this money to the Russian dictator? And don't you think the Russian turns right around and greases his paw with a little thank-you note, a few golf balls stuffed with a lot of *guano*, maybe? I mean, and all this while my relatives in the Dominican Republic, especially my little brother Federico who just had his two goats up and die on him and he's writing me, me, asking me for American dollars when I had to skip last month's rent and my wife just got laid off at the *factoría* in Chinatown...does that tell you something?"

"Yes," answered Arnaldo, trying to piece together the man's reason along a straight line, but feeling more and more disjointed himself by the rumblings inside himself. No matter how many Bacardis he sipped and burned on his tongue, the revelation which he knew he'd brought inside him was not yet to be seen.

"And as far as the women go," continued the man named Hector, "what can you say about a country where, if you knock them around a few times to remind them who the boss is, who the *hombre* of the house is, they stick you in stinking jail for thirty days?"

"But beating your wife is not the way of the Lord," said Arnaldo, who still, although he did not want to be known as a man of God in the Loma Linda Coctel Bar, could not refrain from preaching.

"It may not be," said the Dominican, "but what is a man to do in a country with so many temptations, where the wife knows what the other man can and cannot do and where she holds you up to his light?"

"What other man?" asked Arnaldo.

"Who ever he is. The prick who invites her in while you're out working, stupidly thinking your good, long *pinga* cock can keep her tame and cooking your meals a few nights a week."

"Oh," answered Arnaldo absent-mindedly, digging in his own thoughts, wondering what lay inside that sealed envelope in his head. "But thinking that way about your wife is not the way of the Lord either."

To this, the man named Hector clucked, spat on the floor next to Arnaldo, and then wiped his mouth on the short white sleeve of his Button Your Fly T-shirt. "You have the Lord too much on your mind, *señor*. Maybe you should be thinking more of the real things that are happening in this world of whores and ingrates I'm telling you about."

"Like what?" asked Arnaldo, sipping his rum and tracing the contour of his face on the smoke-filled mirror.

"Like if you don't watch out for your belongings, somebody else comes and takes them. Like if you leave your woman in the street, somebody else comes and picks her up like the broken-down rocking chair you threw out on the sidewalk last week. Like if you're not watching your back every second, *amigo*, some prick will come along and make a cuckold out of you, big time…and then, big *hombre*, watch your big balls rattle like cowbells on your ox and wither. Get my meaning? Yeah, I'm telling you, this is the same here and in the Dominican Republic, but it's worse here, much worse here in Nueva York where women actually turn into whores the minute they start calling themselves American, the minute they step off that American Airlines flight from Santo Domingo, San Juan or Mayagüez."

"Yes," Arnaldo answered, although the man had gone back to his own thoughts and was no longer engaged in conversation, "I believe I get your meaning."

And the meaning which Arnaldo gleaned from the stranger's words was the same that had been sticking to his thoughts like a tick buried under his skin. It was more a presentiment than a real knowledge of how things were; more a veiled revelation he'd been having for weeks. For Jesus had stopped speaking directly to him on the day he pricked open Mejoral's veins and sucked his blood into his mouth to feed his baby daughter. He now communicated only in riddles or in dreams that came across like riddles.

The words of the man were a foreboding that spoke to him of Esmeralda, his sweet Esmeralda, his baby daughter whom he loved with a strange love he had never dared define. It was a love that encompassed the love of a man for his woman, but which to him was also a sacred love such as a man can never feel for a woman *in the natural*, except if that woman be Patricia, an angel sent from God as recompense on the year he was born again and gave his heart to Jesus.

And if anyone—say that district attorney that questioned Juan but not him—would have asked Arnaldo how he, a man of God, justified his nightly apparitions before his daughter, where he exploded at her side with deep and hungry calls, Arnaldo would have answered that he did it for love. It was love for her and for her mother that impelled him to her side. And in all those years he had preserved her virgin swath and revered her on a pedestal like Mary.

And that foreboding he was feeling, that message that was still sealed in a tight envelope on the afternoon he entered the Loma Linda Coctel Bar, rather than rip, began to slowly peel as a letter under steam, unfolding the message Arnaldo wished he'd never read. For the words of the man named Hector, the words of admonition against leaving your woman to be devoured by vultures in the street, this simple fact which every man knows about the moment he feels the stubble on his cheek or the pressing of his member at night against the sheets, came to Arnaldo as the warning he'd purposely strangled in the dark. As the memory of the terrible alarm that exploded in his head that first night when Esmeralda came home like a floating orchid embedded in dreams of Juan.

And with the sounding of that alarm came the terrible notion that Esmeralda, too, as the man had just put it, had turned into an American whore. He felt this despite having no reason to suspect—other than the fact that now that rich *exilado* frequented their church and that since his arrival Esmeralda had blossomed more beautifully than the most radiant red hibiscus in his yard. It was a thought, a terrible notion that he could not confirm, but which had gnawed at him and bit under his skin for weeks, until, like a sleep walker, he brought himself to the Loma Linda Coctel Bar to listen to what Bacardi rum and the cab driver from the Dominican Republic could tell.

"Tell me this, *amigo*," he asked the man named Hector, who was beginning to list at his side and squint his eyes in an effort to focus. "What would you do if you suspected, say, that your woman was a *puta* whore...if you suspected, that is, but had no cause?" Arnaldo at that point was not aware that he thought of Esmeralda as his woman, but rather as a father defending his daughter's honor, which he reasoned, for practical purposes, he could discuss the same way.

And the man, understanding the seriousness and sadness of Arnaldo's intent and in spite of being underwater from his eleventh beer, summoned his most sober persona and acted like the *amigo* he had told him he was. "Well, for starters, I wouldn't go jumping my skin off and tearing my hair out for no reason at all. I mean I wouldn't want to look like a *maricón* in case I'm wrong, if you know what I mean."

"So what would you do to find out if you're right? Or, if you're wrong?" Arnaldo looked into the man's eyes, then focused on the tip of his gray nose.

"For starters," said the man named Hector, "I would ask myself this question: Is she there when I need her? Then I would ask, is she there when I don't need her? If both answers are in the positive, I would say I'm just jerking off and forget about it. Have another *Cuba Libre* or something."

Arnaldo pondered the words of the man, which he was sure now were Jesus' way of slipping him a note under the door without talking to him directly. After a few minutes' consideration, when the man was already starting a baseball conversation with a friend at the other end of the bar, Arnaldo squeezed his shoulder and continued: "What if one of the answers is in the positive and the other in the negative?"

"Which one is the negative?" asked the man, collecting himself in spite of the buzzing in his ears.

"The one about being there when you don't need her."

"Well, in that case, I would find out where she is when I don't need her. But I wouldn't waste too much time on it, you know...because if you waste too much time on it and she finds out you've been wasting time on her and worrying about her and all that stuff, you get demoted in her eyes, if you know what I mean. And then in the end you may lose even if you had no reason to worry in the first place, if you get my meaning."

"No," answered Arnaldo, "I don't quite get your meaning."

"I mean," said the man, looking suspiciously at him, not understanding that Arnaldo had never known the ways between a woman and a man, "that women shouldn't be shown too much concern. If you look weak, the way a man is weak if a woman cuckolds him because, you understand, a *macho* man can never be cuckolded, then later on she will cuckold you anyway, just because you showed her you were a *maricón* who had to worry about whether his woman was his or not to start with. Get it?"

"Yes," answered Arnaldo, "I think so. But tell me then, how would you do it in a way that she would not, as you say, lose respect for you in the end?"

"Why," answered the man named Hector, "I would do it the same way women do it, only they don't tell you. I'd do it the sneaky way, behind their backs, using the same kind of weapons they use on us, the whores."

"Like what?" Arnaldo was following his reasoning, but he wanted to get the last drop.

"Like, for example," said the man, "never ask her directly. The first thing I would do, I guess, is ask her to be there when I don't need her. Surprise her one day. For instance, say, *cariño*, honey, why don't you come over and be with me on such and such a time when you know and she knows you're never there."

"And what if she comes at such a time?"

"Well, in that case," replied the man, "you have to apply the wrestler's double lock. Do you ever watch them on TV?"

"No."

"Trap her good. Pin her down on the canvas and don't let her go until you know for sure."

"How?"

"Well, like for instance, follow her if you have to. Or have your *primo* or your buddy at the *factoría* follow her. Don't let her see you, though. Eventually you'll know. Trust me, *amigo*, you always know."

And those were the words Arnaldo was waiting to hear. For, although he would never explain it to the man named Hector, whom he would never see again, it came to him during this conversation that it was time to uncover what his heart had been hiding from him all these weeks like a dirty dog covering his tracks.

Arnaldo resolved that very moment, with his last sip of Bacardi, to face up to his fears like an *hombre*, even if what lay at the end of that long and winding tunnel brought him a knowledge he could never endure. And although he believed he must first find proof and not be a false accuser or say to his brother Ra-ca or Thou Fool, still the thought of Juan as the man who had defiled his Esmeralda came to him in a flash while the Dominican was counseling him. It came the way he imagined Don Mario Ona had figured out who had made Patricia pregnant while Esmeralda was still swimming like a fish of many colors deep in her mother's womb and not knowing what Arnaldo was feeling or how he loved her mother every night, or that all this was happening in the heart of Cuba, on the cusp of a Revolution that eventually caused a man like Juan to come to these shores in a shiny suit, pretending to look for Jesus when he was actually working for the Enemy.

Eleven

Arnaldo had been classified 111-A during Vietnam—registrant deferred by reason of extreme hardship to dependents—and he'd been grateful that the Lord Jesus had spared him personally the watershed of those early American years. He felt that way because he never would have abandoned Esmeralda. Had he been drafted, he would have had to flee once more. He knew not where this time, perhaps *al norte, más al norte.* He felt that in his short life, at the beginning of the Cuban Revolution, he'd seen enough of bullets that fossilized like scarabs in your belly and shrapnel that spread across the sky and then rained back black blood into your eyes and mouth till you went blind and drowned. He fervently believed that war was waged by the devious, by men who halted between two opinions, speaking for peace and hungering after carnage—calculating men, bloodthirsty men, lovers of the ambush.

During those Vietnam years, when he was more interested in the Bay of Pigs invasion and what

Khrushchev was doing to Fidel than what Lieutenant Calley was in hot water for, Arnaldo knew a *gusano*, a Cuban exile who had enlisted as a marine to fight for Ky. His name was Pedro del Valle, and he had met him by chance one afternoon when he was called to fix a toilet. This Pedro turned out to be the slum landlord of one of the buildings where Arnaldo worked as a handyman.

Pedro was at least thirty, a tall, arrogant man who tipped him generously and seemed to have a soft spot for Arnaldo, perhaps because he pitied Arnaldo being a poor boy of twenty alone in the world, a rootless *yuca* without a pot to piss in or a decent woman to help him raise his daughter. And this Cuban *gusano*, this Pedro del Valle who loved nothing more than to tell Arnaldo tales of how stupid and how evil Fidel was, and who had turned into such a patriotic American in the three or four years he'd been here that he had an American flag as big as a Spanish armoire hanging from the ceiling in the middle of his living room on Fifth Avenue and Seventy-Ninth Street, left for Khe Sanh one early morning with the ARVN 37th Ranger Battalion. Pedro del Valle, a proud Marine ready to do to communism in Southeast Asia what he could not do to it in Havana, Oriente or Pinar del Rio.

A year later, when this proud Yanqui Cubano returned to New York, Arnaldo was called to his fancy apartment. He shared the place with a younger man dressed in fatigues and high, polished black boots and introduced him as his brother, although he had a Puerto Rican accent like the one Arnaldo had heard in the mouth of a sanitation man from Bayamón. When Arnaldo was invited in by the one Pedro called his brother, he found only half a man, for several hundred 122mm rockets followed by artillery and heavy mortar rounds from the Viet Cong had succeeded in taking the rest from Pedro del Valle. That's when Arnaldo first remembered hearing about ambushes and all the military tactics that were suddenly coming to him now as swiftly as the paper airplanes Esmeralda brought home from the boys at PS 155 and chased like butterflies around the house.

"Back in Nam, there were two main types of ambushes," he remembered hearing the poor *gusano* tell him that day, watching the missing part of his body hide under the embroidered Cuban quilt, observing him rise and fall with his arms and his head to make up for all the rest of him that wasn't there. "They were what we called the hasty ambushes and the deliberate ambushes."

"Tell him the difference," Arnaldo remembered the young Puerto Rican man say, helping Pedro del Valle crank up his pride like the metal lever in his wheelchair.

"The hasty ones," Pedro had said back then, "came when we suddenly became aware of the presence of the enemy and grabbed the chance to bush-wack him. We'd get into some sort of last-minute firing line and keep as quiet as possible. And then, when we saw the Commies go by, we'd just grab them by the balls and blow them away!

"The deliberate ambushes," Pedro del Valle had gone on to explain before Arnaldo had finished mounting the full-length mirror he had been called to drill and screw on the ceiling over the bed, "were a lot more complicated and fun.

"First, you'd select a location for your ambush and plan exactly, to the last hair on your chest, what it was you were going to do to the enemy and in how many perverse and different ways you were going to put your *pinga* to him and screw him good. Then on the way there, you'd designate rally points, so if anything went wrong, you'd make it back to those points. After the last rally point, you'd put the site of the ambush under surveillance twenty or thirty minutes. If the coast was clear, you moved your people to your positions and from then on out you just kicked ass, my friend. Believe me, you kicked it high and you kicked it good!"

Remembering the words of the Cuban marine, a deliberate ambush was what Arnaldo was think-ing about the morning he woke up in his bed and found Esmeralda gone before seven, gone before it was her time to check in at the beauty parlor. His first thought was to go straight there. He had the address, although he had never gone because he had not wanted to make Esmeralda ashamed of his dirt-poor peasant face in front of the gentle people, rich women and movie stars she said went there. Still, the thought of a guerrilla ambush, of setting up his own Esmeralda like a Viet Cong, gave him a vertigo twist to the gut, like a spinning top that started in the pit of his stomach and reached all the way to his mouth, churning out little gulps of bitter vomit with the stop-and-go motion of the washer dryer.

"I see." He heard himself repeat the words from the young Spanish-speaking receptionist on the second floor of the beauty salon. "Esmeralda Saavedra has not worked here...she left this job several weeks ago?"

He did not ask where she might be or if the young woman in the black leotards who had three glass earrings dangling on her shoulders had any idea where he could find his daughter. He felt in his gut, still wrenched since he awoke and found her gone, that where she was no one knew but Esmeralda and that young *exilado*, that cunning Don Juan who had called himself a born-again to his face.

Because he could not, as he wanted to, look in every corner, in every apartment building or under every bush in Central Park, Arnaldo decided to wait until that night and then, like that Cuban *gusano* had explained years ago, set his trap, his hasty or his deliberate ambush, whichever the Lord Jesus told him to do.

"How is your job at that beauty parlor, Esmeralda? Do you like it?" Arnaldo asked her at eight o'clock that evening, the moment she returned from her day's tryst with Juan.

Esmeralda did not detect the razor blade in his tongue. Arnaldo had made a deliberate effort to camouflage it and was keeping in mind the advice of the Dominican at the Loma Linda Coctel Bar to never tip his hand.

Esmeralda answered him with the lie she had learned to flex like truth all those weeks, with the half of her cracked coconut she'd learned to place face down.

"It's fine. They treat me fine. I just cashed yesterday's check...put the money in the tin box under your Sunday Bible. Did you find it?"

"Yes."

There was silence while Arnaldo tried to figure out what the Lord Jesus might do next if he found himself in such a situation with his daughter—not that Arnaldo would ever think of Jesus as having an illegitimate daughter, seeing as He never married nor was given in marriage, for to him Jesus was the purest man on earth.

A short time later, while Esmeralda and Arnaldo were still standing in silence in the kitchen that doubled as his bedroom, Arnaldo received a missive that was as clear as when the backyard rooster crows and tears the ceiling of the dawn for the first time. It came to Arnaldo to follow the trail of the young man instead and observe where it led.

"This young man, the *exilado* who comes to church, what is his name...Juan?" Arnaldo started casually.

"Yes, Juan," Esmeralda answered carefully.

"Juan, I know," said the father, "but Juan what? Does he have a last name?"

"Juan Ona."

"Ona, did you say?" Arnaldo felt the blood rush along the sides of his head, opening wide and pounding, as when a tributary finds the wide Caribbean Sea.

"Yes, Ona, I believe," answered Esmeralda, beginning to wonder but ignoring her own doubts. "I believe his family came from Oriente."

Arnaldo, who by then was holding on to his Bible under the table, rubbing the pages blindly, remained as still as he could and tried to muster the equipoise of Paul when he was summoned by the great Agrippa.

"From the Ingenio Ona...was his family from the Ingenio Ona?"

"I think so, Papá. I think he told me his father used to own sugar mills or something, but I'm not sure. It was a long time ago, you know. He came here like me, as a baby. His parents live in Miami and do something else now."

"No," said Arnaldo, speaking into the air in a hollow, disembodied voice, looking like a fly whose wings have just been spun into the spider's web. "I do not remember any Juan at the Ingenio Ona… and I do not remember anyone named Ona who could have had a child named Ona around that time, since Don Mario and Doña María were the only ones."

Esmeralda recognized the names as those of Juan's parents right away, but decided at that moment that the two halves of her coconut were spinning dangerously close.

"Well, I don't know, Papá."

And Arnaldo was left like a man with a puzzle with as many broken pieces as the map of Cuba itself, a puzzle he knew contained the answer whole, but which this time neither Bacardi nor the cab driver at the Loma Linda Coctel Bar could solve.

The following morning, Arnaldo descended the long four flights of their tenement house before dawn and hid in the entrance to the *cuchifrito* store, waiting for the time when he would hear his daughter's unmistakable swift and graceful feet make their way into the early summer's day. He knew now that this would have to be a deliberate ambush, and that to follow her he would have to walk with precision, far enough to go unnoticed and close enough to detect her every step. Far enough to have a bird's eye view and close enough to tell, if she should suddenly turn and find herself in the arms of the man who called himself Juan Ona, which bell she had rung or what knob she had turned.

When the moment came, after the subway ride to Ninety-Sixth Street and the walk through half-deserted streets, Arnaldo saw his daughter suddenly stop before a brownstone and disappear so quickly up the carpeted staircase that he could not tell which intercom button she had pressed or if she owned the key that turned the parlor lock. He knew, though, as sure as rain, that his daughter Esmeralda Saavedra was inside a rich man's house, being savored like a mango, spilling her heart like coconut milk, peeling back her sweet banana skin for that callous infidel to see and swallow whole.

Arnaldo waited, staring at Juan's building from across the street, leaning up against the wall, hoping to catch his daughter's silhouette, hoping for a sign to tell him which wall to scale, which way to go.

And while he waited, he began reciting the Beatitudes the way he had done when he was called to perform his early miracles back home, before he'd lost a whole life and a whole country and the sweet innocence that anointed him and made him into an *hombre de Dios*, as handsome and as strong as the one who called himself Juan Ona and who had turned his Esmeralda into a *puta* whore.

When he got through the Beatitudes, he continued mouthing the verses that followed according to the Gospel of St. Matthew (for he knew it all by heart). All at once, he heard himself speak the words that he finally took for a sign: "And if thy right eye offend thee, pluck it out, and cast it from thee: for it is profitable for thee that one of thy members should perish, and not that thy whole body should be cast into hell." And now Arnaldo needed only to ask Jesus which member he should pluck out and cast from him—whether it be his sweet Esmeralda, corrupted by the lust and the greed of this world, or Arnaldo. For Arnaldo felt offended in himself for the murderous thoughts that welled in him against the *exilado* and the many times he had cursed him and wished him dead and burning in the flames of hell.

To know Arnaldo the way his faithful parishioners knew him and the landlords he worked for remembered him and the way the crew at the sanitation department thought of him was to know a mild and kindly man who was slow to anger and never vindictive, a man who in all ways acknowledged Him who directed his ways. The premeditated actions that followed his discovery of his daughter's betrayal will always seem difficult to understand to those who knew him. To the others who never knew him but merely read about him one morning in *El Diario*, those actions appeared simply as the ways of a jealous man.

As when he loved and played baseball, Arnaldo divided the steps that followed into bases. First base had been when he had caught Esmeralda in a lie. Second base was the day he had followed her, waited for her while leaning up against the wall, and then finally, at the burst of midday, surprised them, his twin children, arm in arm, kissing in the street like dogs in heat, like the mongrels his cousin Perfecto back in Oriente used to say you could only pry apart with buckets of scalding water from the well. Third base was a terrible discovery. Home plate became the boomerang.

After Arnaldo had found them walking arm in arm and had seen Esmeralda, his very own daughter, surrender like a lily under the weight of another man in a way he would never have suspected, for she had never been that way with him during his nightly visitations, a river of thin, hard ice began to overtake him. And rather than a desperate Othello, Arnaldo became a calculating general, a cold surgeon measuring exactly his first and then his last incision to the heart.

"That young man, that Juan Ona, he's your friend, isn't he, Esmeralda?" Arnaldo had asked her on the day following his first discovery while she was preparing his evening meal.

"I see him at church, and you know I've talked with him about the Lord." Esmeralda was beginning to suspect, but at this time she didn't know which way to take.

"When was he born, do you know? Because I used to know some people by his name back in Oriente." Arnaldo had never told Esmeralda Patricia's real last name for fear that someday the Ona dogs would find her in exile or for fear that Esmeralda would find them. And he didn't know when he questioned Esmeralda that evening, as he secretly fantasized gouging Juan's heart out and feeding it to wild dogs up in the Bronx, what twisted knot his words would suddenly untie.

"As it turns out," Esmeralda said with an excitement she could not hide, for it was part of her sweet, spontaneous devotion for her twin, her lover, her other, "Juan and I were born on the same day, the same year, the same time and everything. Isn't that strange?"

She wanted to say much more and felt at that time a deep desire to come clean with Arnaldo, to reveal to him the love she and Juan Ona shared. But the news of their identical birth fell on Arnaldo with such desperate and heavy force that he fainted on the floor, vomiting spontaneously, a high dam overflowing with yellow bile and blood. At that moment, just before he lost consciousness, he understood the meaning of Juan's birth and why

Patricia at three months pregnant looked like nine. And suddenly he saw before him the face of this young man for the first time and understood he was, like Esmeralda, the living image of Patricia. With that thought, Arnaldo passed out at Esmeralda's feet. And she, knowing what to do in the manner the Spirit would direct, dragged him up by his arms onto the sofa bed and spent the evening applying cold compresses of camomile and lemon tea to his ankles and forehead, reading at random from the Bible wherever the pages opened to, singing hymns of praise, and ordering Satan to get behind her and flee from them seven times seven.

In the middle of the night, Esmeralda woke her father up.

"Are you all right now, Papá?" she asked.

"Yes," he answered. But he could barely move a muscle.

The next morning, feeling sure that she could leave Arnaldo to recover by himself, Esmeralda left their apartment in a quick flight to Juan, to their love nest and to their private butterflies. She missed her lover that morning more than ever, and in her heart she had begun to sprout the seed of hope that someday her father would understand and she would lose all fear of leaving Arnaldo and cleave to her lover, her husband, her other and, as Jesus had said, leave father and mother and the whole world behind.

Arnaldo, when he awoke later that afternoon
and found her gone, knew this time what he had to
do. It was clear to him that he should rise and receive his son, his new son, and reveal to Esmeralda
the complete story of her birth. He would lay his
hands on both of them that they repent of the terrible sin that had befallen them. He also blamed himself, for how, he asked, could he not have known
there was another child in the room that terrible
day when he watched the doctor roll Patricia's eyes?
How could he not tell, when Jesus must have hint-
ed at the answer a thousand and one times?

That day, Arnaldo forgot his obligations to the
landlords and the sanitation men and set himself on
his journey to Carnegie Hill, a journey that seemed
like Moses' long march across the desert. Arnaldo
did not go as the man who had loved his daughter in
the dark, or as the jealous lover who despised the
intruder, or even as the minister standing and
thumping on the platform of the Mosaic Decalogue,
but as the father of two children who deserved his
understanding and who were, after all, the living
legacy of his great and only love.

That night after vomiting and passing out,
while Esmeralda slept beside him still clutching the
Bible, Arnaldo had a vision. It was a vision of emerald light and white forgiveness. Jesus came with
Mary Magdalene, and presented him Patricia as she
was then, a girl of seventeen all dressed in white,

calling at his tin- and thatched-roof hut with a cluster of pearl buttons in her hand. With this vision of Patricia clearly hovering above him like an angel, Arnaldo received the gentle peace of understanding he had known during the years just before the Revolution, before the Devil and a new country, hard as slabs of ice where the dead lie, took all his hope.

Arnaldo knew Esmeralda and Juan lay together under what he imagined was a gossamer mosquito netting on the top floor of the house on Madison and Ninety-First. He knew now it was the top floor because his nose, as sure as a divining rod, had led him step by step to his daughter's natural jasmine and cinnamon toast scent all the way up to the blood-red door.

He thought of knocking, as his plan was to come in filled with the Holy Ghost, to reason with them, impart the truth and ask Jesus to lead him in the deep prayer where the Spirit itself can intercede. He felt no anger or remorse at that particular moment, at the moment just before he found his Esmeralda intertwined with the man he still regarded as a stranger, although he understood him now to be his only son.

But as it happened, the door, which Esmeralda had neglected to latch when she came in earlier that day, opened of its own accord. And, suddenly, Arnaldo found himself in the middle of the studio room in front of a brass bed, regarding his daughter and his son in deep and passionate embrace, wrapped in the high moaning of lovers in the chase. They became a pair of startled heads with arched eyes the size of giant beetles. Then they became two solid, naked, flesh-and-sinew silhouettes standing before him with whirling hands. They called out from some deep underwater dream, crying for mercy, hurling themselves into the long screwdriver that quickly turned into a dull and jabbing knife, shucking pink flesh from Juan's rib cage and boring deep wide holes of blood into his heart and lungs.

While Arnaldo continued his disembodied jabbing into Juan with a force as monstrous as a hurricane, his own daughter, his Esmeralda, who'd pried herself from his Herculean foot that had her pinned against the floor, turned on Arnaldo with Juan's painted hammer, the one he used to nail his canvass on the wall. Without reflecting for an instant or asking the Lord Jesus for His help, Esmeralda dealt her father the deadly blow that felt like melting tar on hard cement and split his brown and blood-red coconut head in two.

TWELVE

Whether Esmeralda knew what she was doing at that precise moment she split her father's head in two, opening a long river of blood that washed the studio and dripped slowly and sadly down the long carpeted staircase of the brownstone, was never established by the D.A.

It was evident to the police after seeing Juan's punctured body, barely breathing, wrapped in the red-soaked sheets, with an oxygen mask the paramedic from Mount Sinai had strapped on him like a parachute around the frail wings of a butterfly, that Arnaldo had been killed in an act of self-defense.

"Two lovers," said the detective to the reporter from *El Diario* who came asking around the 19th precinct, "and the woman's father finds them in bed and gets pissed and attacks the guy. Then the guy tries to stop him with a hammer and kills him."

This was the story that Juan, gasping for breath and clinging to Esmeralda's hair like a torn curtain while she phoned 911, insisted she tell. For he did not want the records to show, or history to know, or the Cuban papers in Miami to write that his future wife had been guilty of patricide.

But questions remained. Juan was called down to the station a week later, as soon as the wounds were treated with chicken fat and iodine and wrapped in gauze and linen handkerchiefs (or so it seemed to Esmeralda, who stood beside her brother in the emergency room and answered all the questions from the medics and the nurses as though she were in full command). Arnaldo had punctured Juan from his chest to his groin, but the screwdriver itself had not pierced the vital organs.

"What was Mr. Saavedra doing in your apartment?" was the first question put to Juan.

"I don't know." That was the answer he gave most frequently, hearing his own voice like the faint metallic trill from the two-way radio in the EMS truck just before he saw black.

"Was he aware of your involvement with his daughter?"

"I don't know. I didn't think so."

"How long had you and Ms. Saavedra been seeing each other?"

"Since May."

"What is the nature of your relationship?"

"Engaged...secretly."

"Why secretly?"

"Esmeralda wanted to wait."

"Were you a member of Mr. Saavedra's religious group?"

"I attended a few times."

"Did Mr. Saavedra ever show any animosity towards you or tell you he did not want you to see his daughter?"

"No."

"How did you meet his daughter?"

"By accident. I stumbled into their Sunday service one morning."

"Had you ever heard about or had any previous knowledge of Mr. Saavedra or his daughter before that day?"

"No. Why?"

"Were you aware that there was an outstanding warrant for Mr. Saavedra in connection with his abduction of a child from Cuba and transportation of said child to the United States under false declarations to the Immigration authorities in the State of Florida?"

"No...what child? As far as I know Esmeralda is his only daughter."

"Precisely. And were you aware that the parties who originally filed the claim in 1962 were a Mr. and Mrs. Mario Ona, said individuals bearing your same last name?"

"No...those are my parents... No, I didn't know anything about it at all.... Say, what *is* this? This sounds crazy!" A red alarm had gone off in

Juan's head, as loud as the one that had exploded in Arnaldo's ears that first day when Juan and Esmeralda lay together for the first time in the abandoned crack house on One Hundred and Eleventh Street.

Juan's grandparents had never told him about filing charges for an abducted child when they came to America. They had told him that a terrible thing involving a little girl had befallen them at the onset of the Castro revolution. They had said it was a deed so black and cruel that they had kept it a secret from him and all their friends and that they could never bring themselves to speak of it.

All during his growing years, Juan had assumed the dastardly deed—as Don Mario labeled it and referred to it the few times he mentioned it— involved the murder of the child of one of the *campesinos* at the Ingenio Ona. Juan had tucked it in his memory as one of the many Cuban tales of woe he'd heard Don Mario and scores of other Cuban exiles tell.

"So, in your opinion, would Mr. Arnaldo Saavedra have objected to your involvement with his daughter?" continued the interrogator.

"No, I didn't think he would have objected that much eventually, when he got to know me... But, obviously, he did."

But the young assistant D.A., with a yarmulke bobby-pinned like a tonsure to his head, did not think the case so obvious. Juan waived his right to have a lawyer present and was kept at the precinct with detective Ramírez and assistant district attorney Hausler for three more long hours. And the questions persisted because Hausler could not get in his head that Arnaldo would have just let himself in and without threat or provocation would have attempted to murder the boyfriend of the woman he said was his daughter. After all, Esmeralda was twenty-nine years old; not a minor nor mentally or physically handicapped. Juan could not explain Arnaldo's behavior any more than the young assistant district attorney himself.

Under the pressure of interrogation, Juan suddenly began vomiting profusely, shooting up yellow bile like a geyser into the thick precinct air. Detective Hausler called an ambulance and sent Juan back to Mount Sinai, where he remained under care and observation for another long and anxious week.

Everyone who knew Esmeralda believed they would find her at the apartment in a black dress surrounded by candles and Arnaldo's sad belongings. When the parishioners finally learned of his tragic leap into the arms of Jesus, they were initially afraid to call on her because they multiplied her grief ten times theirs and calculated it impossible that a young woman who had been the golden light and whole heart of her father, a young woman who had been true and devoted with the fervor of a saint, could possibly endure such pain. But when they finally called, there was no Esmeralda there.

For days, the apartment on One Hundred and Seventeenth Street lay vacant, as when a ghost who was betrayed or suffered an untimely death finally leaves the haunted house.

Juan, who was not visited once during his week at Mount Sinai and who from his hospital bed hired a man from Pinkerton to search for his beloved, grew weaker and despondent believing that Esmeralda, under the unbearable knowledge of her act, had lost her mind or taken her own life or simply disappeared into the night like a wounded animal, sparing her pack the misery of her demise.

The place no one thought to look—not the Pinkerton man nor detective Ramírez's man, who wanted answers he could not get from Juan—was in the cordoned off apartment on Madison and Ninety-First. There, the chalk still traced Arnaldo's fallen silhouette and bitter-wine blood still soaked the floor. And there Esmeralda lay frozen under the brass bed, trembling with fear the way she used to while waiting for her father's visitations in the dark.

The two weeks since Arnaldo's murder had been for Esmeralda like centuries, or like the slide that inevitably got stuck in the projector during art class at Julia Richman High School and repeated and repeated its image on the screen.

But the things that had festered in Esmeralda's eyes—the soft tar on her father's head, the caving in, the blood—could not compare with the terrible truth she learned from the young man with the yarmulke bobby-pinned in the middle of his head.

The first sign that there were carnal weapons turned against her came when Esmeralda could no longer summon her butterflies or entertain her lizard friends or lift herself above the fear of things she could not accept with her reasoning mind. She believed that not only had her father been taken from her by reason of her terrible act, but that with him had flown away her Ghost and Morpho butterflies, escorting and chasing Arnaldo into the arms of Jesus, leaving her like an abandoned chrysalis in the middle of New York.

The second sign came with the detective and the young district attorney forming an acute angle in her path on the day Juan had been questioned and then rushed to the hospital.

"And did you know that Mr. and Mrs. Mario Ona, Juan Ona's parents, had filed a complaint that Mr. Saavedra had abducted their daughter from Cuba...the day she was born...brought her to the State of Florida...false information to the immigration officials...standing warrant for his arrest in that state...1962."

The young district attorney's information was incomplete, and there were many missing pieces of the puzzle which she could not juggle precisely into place. But Esmeralda, even in her sad and frozen state, realized that Juan, her beloved, her other, whom the parishioners had told her time and time again looked exactly like her, was more than her twin soul. He was in fact her twin.

On the fifteenth day after the murder, while Arnaldo still lay frozen because Esmeralda had not gone to claim the corpse—for she believed him gone to Jesus with her butterflies—Juan returned home to pack his suitcase. He meant to check in at the Carlyle, since he could not think of staying any longer in that blood-stained spot where he had lost his Esmeralda. But his heart now told him the minute he entered the apartment that she was alive. And if she was, then he had faith that he could find her, or that somehow the butterflies or her sweet Jesus would bring her back to him intact.

And what Juan found when he leaned over and reached under the box spring, looking for a sketchbook he kept tucked under the bed, was a frozen butterfly, Esmeralda, closed wings like a dim moth, thin and desiccated from immovable days of thirst and fast.

Overcome, Juan pulled her out and held her in his arms, breathing his breath of life into her, folding her chest in his like a mother hen, covering her with the wide wings of his love. He spat in her mouth, the way Arnaldo had done long ago on that

leaky boat in Cuba, and forced water into her with
the turkey baster he used to mix his paints, and
soaked her forehead and her body—her still beautiful cinnamon body—and whispered words of life
into her ears and pillowed hair.

When Esmeralda finally responded, it was with
a faint moan like the rustle of silk. She was in
Juan's arms in the cab on their way to Lenox Hill
Hospital—Juan never wanted to see Mount Sinai
again. And because Esmeralda, as only Arnaldo had
known, had always been a child with supernatural
powers of recovery, it wasn't long before she was
renewed and Juan could speak with her and hold
her hand at her bedside in the hospital. Soon they
reveled in each other's sight—a gift which Esmeralda understood immediately upon awakening had
not left her, in spite of the dark knowledge she now
had, in spite of her grief and the violent act she
could never look squarely in the eye or even accept
as being entirely true.

"I would like for us, as soon as you feel a little
stronger, Esmeralda, to go back to Miami and settle
there," was the way Juan began, tentatively, careful
not to bruise the gentle mango or bring back the
dark thoughts that had hurled her under his bed for
one whole week.

"I've never been to Miami," answered Esmeralda, pulling up her mechanical bed.

"Well, we flew over it once, remember? You said you liked the backyard pools and the sailboats." Juan heard himself cajoling her as one cajoles a child who has not drunk his milk. He knew Esmeralda would detect the condescension but never call him on it. She was a Cuban to the bone, as Arnaldo had made her, and shunned the ways of direct confrontation.

"But going to Miami will not be so easy, Juan," she said, slightly prying open the lacquer box that contained the secret with a tentative motion that could let it be shut quickly once again. They now shared the dark secret but had not dared approach it.

Her emerald eyes had received their burnished light from heaven once again, and she caressed Juan with them, bathing him with a tenderness that gave him the courage to proceed. He had feared this moment and was unsure how much Esmeralda had been told by Hausler or if she knew anything at all. And all the while, during the many days he had entertained these thoughts, wondering how they would pour the new wine into old bottles, he had not arrived at the answer he was seeking until that very moment when Esmeralda opened the secret box and let the genie out that could lead them, step by step, into the hairpin road of their future, where Juan took the curves blindly, not knowing what was on the other side, holding on to Esmeralda who was coiled around him like a snake.

"But it can be…if we can paint over certain things, cover them with mother-of-pearl white, paint a vase of flowers or a seascape in place of all those things that would try to rend our love asunder." Juan had used the Bible word *asunder* knowing that Esmeralda could always be reached that way, the way her poor benighted father taught her.

At first he feared that Esmeralda would be troubled by the obvious, by what he called the elephant in the living room, which is to say the matter of their twin births and the injunction in Leviticus and the sins of the fathers being visited upon five generations. But the genie she had let out of that lacquer box was leading her along a completely different path.

"But in Miami, what would you tell Don Mario and Doña María that my name is? And what about my father?"

Juan, astonished and yet elated at the practical turn her mind had taken, now felt free to speak his heart. For all during those days after Hausler's revelation, he had done nothing but consider their fate. And every time he tried to imagine his life without her, a deep melancholy and a fierce fear would overtake him. He concluded that his love for her—and hers for him—must override all things and contain what he knew in his heart seemed uncontainable. In the hospital, he had remembered a Mexican tune which he used to rock himself to sleep when there was trouble or when his roommate's television kept him up at night:

> Me he de comer esa tuna
> me he de comer esa tuna
> aunque me raje la mano.
>
> (I will eat that cactus
> even if it splits my hand in two)

"We will say that your name is something else," he began. "Let's say Esmeralda Mendoza, for example, like your friend the lizard... and that your parents died, say, in a car crash in the Catskills, and that they were Mexican Americans. My folks will have no trouble believing that. And they'll like you, of course they will."

They were holding each other with both hands, unaware of the nurse's aide standing beside them and the chicken soup and Jello pudding wheeled in for Esmeralda's dinner that night. They had been whispering as if to keep their secret even from themselves. Then came the question Juan knew had been hanging like a dagger.

"Do you think Don Mario and Doña María are our parents... or do you think..."

Juan traced her pomegranate lips with his finger tip, as if to silence her, and he kissed her. She did not move or kiss him back, for she was intent on his answer.

"I do not think so," he finally said, drawing a deep sigh that made his stomach swell and the veins on his neck trace their course. "I think probably Patricia was our mother and Arnaldo our father."

He had let out the knowledge he had pieced together and there was no relief in it. Saying it didn't make it go away, and knowing it cast a large spider's web on them, a web—although he would never tell Esmeralda—from which he feared their feet would never be untangled.

"What makes you say that? I thought the same thing!"

Esmeralda was surprised that Juan had arrived at that conclusion, since Hausler's information had been spotty and this idea had come to her in a dream at the hospital, a dream in which Patricia appeared in a silver sequined dress with a mermaid's tail, and Arnaldo mounted her like a horse and floated with her among the morning stars. It was a dream that had given her hope, hope that her father was well and finally reunited with her mother, hope that he had understood the actions of the hammer she could not control, and hope that perhaps now her butterflies would start their descent to earth and bring back her powers of travel in the unseen world.

"It's just some bits of information I pieced together," answered Juan. "Like the fact that my parents...that's what they are to me...told me I had an older sister, Patricia, your mother's name, who died around the time I was born. And other things, things that I guess, as you would put it, the Spirit made known to me somehow. Things I just feel…"

"So…if that's the case," said Esmeralda staring out the hospital window, trying to make even the little pieces fit, "why would your parents put out a warrant to have my father arrested, when he was my father, for real?"

Juan knew that no matter how much their souls were one, or how much their hearts and lives were intertwined with the purest love of all, the one they suckled even before their one became two, Esmeralda would never understand the ways of the wealthy *patrones* back at the Ingenio Ona. There, people as well as oxen and houses and acres and acres of sugar cane all belonged to only one man. There, a simple peasant like Arnaldo could never call anything his own, really his own, much less the daughter or the grandchild of the biggest *hacendado* of all.

"I think Don Mario Ona probably felt that he would provide a better home for you. He's very serious about his grandchildren…. Look how he spoiled me." Juan gave it his best shot and hoped Esmeralda would let it go.

"But Juan," she said after a pause he had learned to identify as Esmeralda's way of letting the Spirit sow the words and wave the railroad flag, "maybe it's better if we stay in New York. We have everything here, don't we?"

"Including grief, Esmeralda...which we should put aside... And then there's something else, these bothersome people, Hausler and that detective Ramírez. I think it's best to leave them behind."

And with those words, Juan summoned up her poor dead father before her and the day she could not stop the hammer in her hand, and the knowledge of their past, which Esmeralda wished with all her heart she'd never heard the government man tell at all. She did not answer Juan, and that day they shut the secret box she had opened for an instant. And together they made a silent covenant to lock that box for all eternity and someday toss the key into the wide Caribbean Sea, along with her dark knowledge of what her father had done with the remains of the orphan boy named Mejoral, and with her memories of Arnaldo naked in the dark, and with the remembrance of that early afternoon when she finally chose between her father and her lover.

Two months after Esmeralda had left the hospital, a lavish civil ceremony was held at the Hotel Fountainbleau in Miami Beach, followed by a Catholic wedding in the Cuban church in Coral Gables. The bride's name was reported in the papers as Esmeralda Mendoza, and the groom, Juan Ona, was happily photographed at her side with his proud parents, Mr. and Mrs. Mario Ona, distinguished members of the Cuban American community, at the helm of the grand event.

The photograph and lengthy article, in which the bridegroom's long list of accomplishments was cited and the bride's exquisite beauty touted to the hilt, ran in *El Nuevo Herald*. And, as Arnaldo had taught his daughter on his knee, *nothing is hidden that shall not be revealed*, the same article was picked up by *El Diario* in Nueva York, because among the many feathers in Juan Ona's cap was the fact that he'd lived briefly in New York and had been commissioned by the mayor for a private portrait of his family.

Among the curious who read the article in *El Diario* were the man named Hector, who never knew Esmeralda was the woman Arnaldo had referred to when he asked for his advice, and detective Ramírez, who translated it for Hausler and then, tossing it aside, told himself he never read the story. Another was Ricardo Maldonado, Arnaldo's parishioner who was a carpenter by trade and who had won two-thousand dollars in the *bolita* with the numbers Juan had given him the day he and Esmeralda met. And there were the nine other faithful followers of Arnaldo who understood immediately there was, as they put it, a rat in the cellar—for they knew Esmeralda Saavedra's name like their own, that it was not Mendoza, and they also knew Arnaldo was not violent, that he never drank and would not plunge a screwdriver into a man without good cause. They also knew that Esmeralda, the girl they knew so well and prayed and praised the Lord with, would never marry in a church that belonged to the Pope unless she was beaten, gagged and chloroformed.

And these nine faithful parishioners understood that someone had been tricked, and they reasoned that the rich *Cubano* had worked the ways of fornication and other deceitful lusts to win over the heart of their sweet Esmeralda. They gathered together one Sunday in His name, hoping that Jesus would be there in the midst of them to tell them what to do, for Arnaldo's sake.

But Ricardo Maldonado, who since winning *la bolita* had become the leader of the group, persuaded them that there was nothing they could do. For who would listen to them, poor *hispanos* without a pot to piss in, *hispanos* who only had Jesus to lean on, while the *exilado* in the shiny suit had *guano* and more *guano*, *chavos* and more *chavos* to buy the whole world on the installment plan if he chose to.

The young couple written about in *El Nuevo Herald* settled in a Mizner house in Key Biscayne not far from Doña María and Don Mario Ona, and it was reported that among the bride's hobbies was collecting exotic butterflies, and that the bride and groom planned a trip to the Amazon in early June.

It was not reported, for there would be no one to tell or understand, that two months after the wedding, Esmeralda had once again been visited by her butterflies, who this time changed their course and transported her due north over One Hundred and Seventeenth Street.